Nyctophobia:

Another anthology of horror

Leabharlanna Poiblí Chathair Baile Átha Cliath
Dublin City Public Libraries

Bradley L. Bodeker

ISBN: 1533351465
ISBN-13: 978-1533351463

FORWARD

In 2014, after the release of my first novel, *Zechariah 14:12-humanity's last stand* I promised my readers a new anthology of horror and hopefully something more improved; I failed to deliver.

There were quite a few life changes I had gone through. I did a vision quest out in Pipestone, MN with a Ojibwe medicine man I had met. It was a huge overhaul of my way of thinking. A spiritual awakening, you might say.

Also, I was dealing with a separation from my wife which turned into a divorce. I packed up and moved to the Twin Cities where I went through several career changes and admittedly, I still am. In the course of all these changes, I did manage to type out a few stories, but nothing I had a fever for until recently.

I live on a nice little hobby farm, a new relationship, kids graduating college and getting driver's licenses. With that being said, I believe I've finally reached what the Eagles once coined "a peaceful, easy feeling".

My mind gets so scattered when it comes to writing. I develop a story, I begin to sketch it out, I start to write it and then another story pops into my head. So I begin to sketch that out, then write it, then another idea pops into my head. The cycle just goes on and on until I have to yell at my brain to knock it off and get in line. "Okay, boys, whose story needs to be told first?" Well, of course they all think they do, and for the most part I can tell these stories through shorts. When those get built up, I release them in formats like an anthology.

Like the first anthology, *Midnight Snacks*, these stories are all ideas that kept crowding my head from when I was a punk teenager to present. *Running Alone* is the very first story I ever wrote, it's been extremely tweaked, but the characters and setting are the same. Also in this book is the long awaited sequel to *Zechariah 14:12*. I wasn't going to write a sequel, but there was a demand for it, so I hope I didn't let you down. I actually was going to write a prequel, but the source material became so immense that I couldn't contain it in a short story. So that will become a novel.
So please, let me thank you, dear reader; for your patience. I so very much appreciate you and your constant support. I know I will never become the

next Stephen King, Clive Barker or H.P. Lovecraft; but I don't write to be famous. I write because I have a story to tell. I write because I like to hear the readers say things like:

"Damn, Brad, you come up with some messed up shit."

"Are you taking your medication?"

"What sort of nightmare's do you have?"

It's comments like that, that encourage me to write more. So please, keep reading. There's something on the road ahead. It might have teeth. It may have tentacles. It may look like an innocent child. But we know better than that. C'mon....you first....

Bradley L. Bodeker 2016

CONTENTS

ACKNOWLEDGMENTS

A special "thank you" to everyone who is holding a copy of this in your hands or on your kindle. I hope you enjoy the ride and please leave a review at Amazon.com.

BACK ROADS

I used to live in a little town called Ceylon, MN. It was 10 miles from the nearest town of Fairmont. I took back roads to and from work. One hot day in July I picked up a woman and her 12-year-old girl who were hitch hiking. It was a nightmare. Not to the extent of this story, but I must admit I was pretty damn scared.

"It's fucking hot, Ronnie!" Gerald spat into his Blackberry, "It's like 112 degrees with the sun beating off the tarmac today! I'm gonna start traveling at night during these summer tours."

He was driving his '68 Olds Cutlass. He had restored her from a junkyard husk to the rolling beauty she is today. Only he didn't fix the motor for the rag top yet, and there was no air conditioning.

"Stop for ice cream." His literary agent said, "You should be coming up on Le Mars, Iowa. It's the 'Ice Cream Capital of the World'."

"I passed Le Mars about 12 miles south already. I'm about 48 miles from the Minnesota border on Highway 60."

His agent spoke again but it was choppy and incomprehensible. He checked his phone and there was a circle with a slash through it. "no service".

"Goddammit!" he said throwing his phone to the seat next to him.

He turned on his radio in which he had a choice of country, the gospel hour, or country. He cursed again and popped a cigarette in his mouth and lit it with the car lighter.

He filled up when he reached Worthington, Minnesota and bought himself an ice cream sandwich and another pack of camel blues. He didn't like taking Interstates because they were usually rerouted away from scenery, little towns with character, etcetera. I-90 sat ahead of him and he looked at his road map. There was a small township road that would take him the same route east and he decided that's what he needed to get to his destination in Rochester, Minnesota where he had a book signing at Barnes and Noble and then it was on to the Mall of America after that in Minneapolis. So he wanted a little rustic atmosphere before he joined suburbia.

County Road 7 stretched on for an hours' worth of farms and fields full with yellowing corn and soybeans. The weather had been dry this summer and crops weren't quite growing to potential. When he drove into Moon Valley County he passed a hog lot every other mile. The stench was so strong he could taste it and ended up finishing a 2-liter bottle of Mountain Dew just to get the taste away.

A half hour later a sharp curve came up dividing two lakes to the north and to the south. Just on the other side of the curve a woman stood on the road with what he figured to be her daughter of about 12 holding an umbrella. The mother had her thumb out.

As his car approached them he noticed sweat drenching both of them making their shirts stick to their skin. The daughter was crying and the mother looked miserable in this heat.

"Don't do it, Ger." His subconscious spoke in his head, "If she was hot or her daughter was a hot 19-year-old? Then maybe. But not them. Not them, Ger. Jesus, the mother looks like she fell off the ugly tree and hit all the branches coming down. You're slowing down, Ger, what the hell are you doing? What are you thinking?"

"It's fucking scorching out!" he scolded himself and found he was slowing down and pulling off to the gravel shoulder.

The mother and daughter were running to the car.

"Too late now, Ger." His subconscious confirmed, "You're committed now."

He cleaned off the passenger seat and moved his duffel bag he always traveled with from the right side of the back seat to the left. He was scooping his discarded McDonald's wrappers off the floor when the mother opened the door.

"How far you going?" the mother asked.

She was a short frumpy woman, with ratty wiry charcoal colored hair. He could see now that she didn't have any front teeth, top or bottom. The daughter was sniffing in her former sobs and clinging to her mother and staring at him distrustfully. She was dirty blonde with slate gray eyes; Skinny as a rail and riddled with acne. Both were wearing jeans with short sleeved shirts.

"I'm heading all the way to Rochester." He answered.

"Gooder." She mumbled and brought the seat forward so her daughter could climb in and then she dropped herself onto the passenger seat with a huff and the car rocked, "If you could drop us off in Enderson Grove I would be so grateful."

"How far is that?" he asked putting the car in gear as they buckled.

"'Bout 27 miles down the road. On the way fer you." She grinned.

As they started down the road he noticed the sour smell of body odor. Musky and heavy. He was thankful the windows were down but wasn't sure if the hog lots were worse than them.

"Kind of hot to be hitchhiking isn't it?" he asked.

"Ain't got any other way to get my baby and go back home. I don't drive and my baby was at her grandparent's house, my mom and dads, and this is the only way I could get her."

"Couldn't you take a bus or somethi---"

"Bus costs $5. I don't have $5."

"Well, good thing I came along then." He smiled at her.

"Yep."

"I have a dishabillatee." Her daughter spoke from the backseat.

"What?" he looked into the rear view mirror.

"I have a dishabillatee." She repeated, "I get real sick when it's hot."

"That's why I brought the umbrella." Her mother spoke up.

"Momma, I'm thirsee." She whined.

"Do you have any pop?" the mother asked.

Gerald looked around on the floor of the passenger side for a bottle of water he had down there. It sat right next to a meaty ankle that was shoved into a pair of flip flops. He reached down for it and her foot moved and brushed against his hand. He pulled the bottle up quickly, almost clumsily.

"Ooops, hehehehe." The mother blushed.

"Ah…" he flustered and composed himself handing the bottle back to the girl, "I've got water I just bought in Worthington?"

The girl grabbed the bottle and threw it out the window, "I doan like wadder!!"

"MINDEEE!" the mom scolded, "you apologize to the nice man!"

"That's alright. I'm not a big fan myself."

"I want pop!" Mindy demanded.

"Sorry, honey." Gerald said calmly, "That's all I got."

She began to pout.

"Is there a town coming up? I can stop and pick up some soda for her." He offered.

"Nope." The mother answered, "Ain't nothin' till you get to Enderson Grove, mister."

"Gerald." He said holding out his left hand, "Gerald Daugherty."

The mother looked at his hand and shook it lightly, "What kind of a man shakes hands with his left hand?"

"Um. Just me, I guess." He said with a nervous chuckle.

"I'm Mary and that's my daughter Mindy."

"Nice to meet you." He lied.

Judging by the first 5 minutes of this ride he was regretting picking them up. He thought the mother was a loser of a parent and the daughter? Well, maybe she has a disability, but she's a damn brat.

"What do you do, Mr. Daugherty?" Mary asked.

"I..uh…I write books."

"Books? You mean like an author? I don't read much books, and the ones I do read are them harleyquin romances. Do you write romances, Mr. Daugherty?"

"Nope. I write horror fiction mostly. Ever heard of *The Ancient* or *Crawlers*? Those were my bestsellers. The first one is being passed around Hollywood for a possible movie."

"Never heard of them, sorry. You should write romances. Women like romances."

"I don't have a romantic bone in my body, just ask my ex-wife." He joked.

"Oh, I bet you're romantic. Most of you creative type of people are."

Gerald grunted.

Other than the incessant whining from the back seat of being "thirsee", there was no communication. He did notice Mary was staring at him. From his peripherals he could make out her big moon face aiming her gaze into his head.

"So you're divorced?" she spoke up.

He sighed, "Yep."

"I can't seem to find a good man. They always end up heavy drinkers or they never stay around long enough. Once you give it up, they leave."

Gerald winced, thinking about anyone wanting to "do the deed" with his passenger.

"It sure gets lonely." She murmured.

More silence and awful mental pictures. He kept looking for road signs saying "Enderson Grove 2 miles". The only thing he saw was seed brand signs. He pushed on the accelerator a little harder.

About a quarter of a mile down the road, Mary grabbed his hand which was resting on the gear shift. It made him jump and snatch his hand away. Mary looked a little hurt but then a grin came to that big doughy face.

"I was only admiring your hands." She said, "You have such masculine hands."

"Um, thanks." Gerry said with his face turning red.

"Why, did I make you blush? Oh, Gerry, you're like a shy little school boy."

Her hand went down and began to touch his thigh just above the knee. He pulled the car off the road into a lot where three large grain elevators stood. There were no trucks around.

"Look, dammit!" he said sharply, "I don't know what you think you're doing but I would appreciate it if you would keep your hands to yourself!"

Mary looked as if she had been slapped. Her eyes watered but no tear fell.

"POP!!" Mindy said from the back seat.

When the dust cleared Gerry saw that she was pointing at a soda machine that was near the weigh house.

"What kind do you like, Mindy." He asked.

"You don't have to." Mary said.

"But, mama, I'm so thirsee!"

"What kind do you like?" Gerry repeated.

"Grape!" she shouted.

"What if they don't have grape?"

"I want grape!"

"Mindy, this is a pop machine in the middle of nowhere; the chances are slim that they have grape."

"Orange!"

"Oh for fuck's sake!" he muttered and then got out of the car.

With some good luck on his side, there was Orange Crush. He put his $1.50 in and Mary spoke up behind him making him jump.

"They had orange?" she asked.

"Um, yep." He said.

"I'm sorry."

"For what?"

"You know. I touched…"

"Forget about it. It never happened, okay? Let's get you and your kid to Emerson's Oak or wherever and we'll never know the wiser."

"Enderson."

"What?"

"It's 'Enderson Grove'. Not 'Emerson Oak'."

"Whatever."

Gerry started toward the car but Mary stopped him.

"We need to talk about this." Mary said.

"There's nothing to talk about, can we go?"

She pouted on her way back to the car. When they both got in, Mindy squealed with delight as Gerry handed her the soda. She began laughing maniacally until Mary reached back and struck her with an open-handed slap.

"Stop acting like a fucking animal!!" Mary screeched.

As Mindy began to cry, Gerry started the car.

"You didn't have to do that." he said.

"Don't tell me how to raise my child, Mr. Daugherty!" she spat, "Mr. High-and-mighty author! You don't even have children do you??"

"Well, no...but.."

"Exactly! Don't pretend to know what it's like to raise a child with Mindy's needs! You don't know squat! I've spent the last 12 years doing nothing but sacrificing for her! 12 fucking years, Mr. Daugherty!! 12 years without a man around to help me out! You don't know what it's like!"

As they got back onto the road, Gerry didn't say a word. He wanted to dump them both off in a corn field somewhere. But after hearing this he felt horrible for even thinking like that. Of course she was lonely and frustrated. He couldn't imagine what her life must be like, and judging by the look of her he thought it must have been pretty rough.

"I'm sorry, Mary." He said finally, "I'm so used to being on my own...I just..."

"I don't expect someone like you to understand."

"You're right. I don't. Can we still be friends?"

A smile lit up her face.

"Do you mean that, Mr. Daugherty?"

"Didn't I ask you to call me 'Gerry'?"

They both had an uncomfortable laugh but things were a little less awkward.

By the grace of all road gods, Enderson Grove was 2 miles ahead. Gerry let out a sigh and lightly punched the accelerator. There was a butcher on the right hand side of the road and then an abandoned old marina.

"That's odd." he said more to himself than anyone else in the car.

"What's odd?" Mary asked.

"A marina, in the middle of nowhere. Are there lakes around here?"

"There's a couple slews, Jacobsen's and Abbey's. But those are shallow, think Abbey's is almost dried up. Most people around here go boating and fishing in Fair Lake."

"Guess that's why business was bad and they closed, huh?"

"Oren was handed that business by his daddy. Used to have a booming business. Then we went through a drought in this part of Minnesota and business dried up."

"Man, that's rough."

"Oren was a pig of a man. A couple nights at 'The Legend', he tried puttin' his dick in me!"

"Should you be talking like that in front of your daughter?" Gerry asked looking in his rear view at Mindy.

"There you go again," Mary's voice trembled. "Telling me how to act in front of my kid!"

"Sorry."

"Just pull over here."

The main street consisted of a feed mill, an abandoned gas station, an antique store, and a bar. On top of said bar was a badly hand-painted sign that read "The Legend". This was where Mary wanted Gerry to pull in at.

"At the bar?" he asked.

"Yes," she said matter-of-factly. "the bar! We live in the apartment above!"

Gerry got out and opened the passenger side door for her.

"I don't need you to open the door for me!" she snapped and then, "C'mon, Mindy, let's go; we're home!"

"Look, Mary," He began. His subconscious began hammering at him again.

She stopped and turned to him. She looked so pathetic, dirty and sweaty. He couldn't imagine the horrors this woman had seen.

"Mary, I apologize at how rude I must have seemed to you and your daughter. Can I at least buy you a drink inside?"

"You want to buy me a drink, Mr. Daugherty?" she said staring at him without trust.

"Please, it's the least I could do."

Mary handed Mindy her bags and slapped her on her ass, "Take these up, and wait for mama to come up."

"Yes, momma." Mindy answered obediently and ran up the rotted wooden staircase to their apartment.

Mary went to open the door to the bar and Gerry grabbed the door for her. She stopped him before they could go in.

"Be warned, Gerry." She said with a blank emotionless moon face, "This is a rural local bar. The boys in here have no time for strangers because they believe this is their own personal playground. A good number of men in this hole feel the same way about me, that I'm their own personal playground. They won't take kindly to you."

"Sounds like the bar from Star Wars." he joked.

"I'm not kidding around. This is the real world, Mr. Author. You may find yourself in a position you can't write yourself out of."

"I'll be fine."

When they walked into the front door it was like a movie set. Everyone inside went silent and stared with intensity at the stranger in their bar. It was hard for his eyes to adjust in the almost too dim atmosphere.

As they sat up at the bar with every eye on them, the bartender walked slowly up to them. He was stout with a deep farmer's tan. Stubble riddled his heavily lined face.

"Who the fuck is this, Mary?" He asked not taking his eyes off Gerry.

"Gerald Daugherty." she said without looking up from the bar,

"He was kind enough to give me and Mindy a ride home from my parent's place. He's a famous author."

"Famous?" The bartender questioned.

"Well, maybe not around here." Gerry said nervously, "But I've got a pretty wide audience in New England."

"Well, I ain't never heard of you."

"Can we get a couple drinks, Hank?" Mary asked, "Or are you just going to stare us down?"

The bartender popped the top off a Coors Light and handed it to Mary, "What are you drinking?"

"Uh...." Gerry eyed the supply of booze behind the bar, noting that Jameson's and Bushmills were scarce. "How about a Seagram's and seven?"

"How about a Canadian and Sprite?"

"That'll work."

They took the first few sips off their drinks and the patrons returned to their own drinks.

Gerry noticed that Mary was staring at him again. He felt those beady eyes gazing at him from his peripherals. He glanced towards her and gave a quick smile and then returned to the small television broadcasting a Vikings game.

"You're ascairt of me, aintchoo, Mr. Daugherty?" she asked.

Without looking, he could tell there was a toothless predatory smile wedged into that fat doughy face of hers.

"Scared?" he let out a nervous chuckle, "No. Why would I be scared of you?"

He slammed the rest of his drink and motioned for a fresh one. A scowl from the bartender and a new drink appeared.

"I can tell. Shit, I can almost smell it on ya."

He laughed to himself. "That smell, my dear." he thought to himself, "Is your own B.O."

"You ain't got nothin' to fear from me, Gerry; I'm a little rough around the edges but I'm just a woman. A lonely woman."

He emptied his glass again, looked down and saw there were only two sips taken from her bottle.

"Well," he said standing up, "I should go. I have a long drive ahead of me. Have to be in Rochester by---"

"Nonsense!" Mary interrupted, "Have another, Gerry. Come on. Hank, get my famous young boyfriend another one over here!"

"Really, Mary, thanks. But I really need to---"

She grabbed his forearm like a crocodile would grab its prey and pulled him close. Her uni-brow furrowed a darkness in those little rat eyes.

"You'll sit down right there, Gerry." she whispered, "Or I'll tell everyone in this bar that you tried to rape me. Better yet, that you tried to rape Mindy. How well do you think that'll fly in this joint, Gerry? How many paces to the door do you think you'll get?"

"What?" He said with a bit of fear trying to betray his otherwise calm demeanor, "Why are you doing this? Seriously, I have to---"

"Hank!" she yelled at the bartender.

"No!" Gerry pleaded, "Wait, Mary! Don't!"

"Hank, guess what this wanna-be famous writer did to little ol

Mindy?" She continued.

Hank walked over to the front of them eying up Gerry again.

"What did he do?" Hank asked not taking his gaze off Gerry.

Gerry began to sweat, knowing that he would never make it to the door if this repugnant piece of shit spat out a lie to these troglodytes.

"He stopped and gave Mindy a pop because she was so thirsty. You know how Mindy gets when she's thirsty."

"Boy, do I ever."

"Can you pour my heroic friend here another drink?"

Gerry let out a deep sigh. Mary reached over and put her meat hooks on his thigh again and rubbed him from the crotch to his knee and then gave a hard squeeze to his knee. He tried to pull away but she gripped him like a steel trap.

"Play along, Gerry." she whispered to him.

"I..." he cleared the knot in his throat, "I have to...go to the men's room."

She turned to face him. He truly did have to use the men's room, but he could not look into her dead stare.

"Then go, dumbshit." she said with a smile, "Or do you need mama to hold your hand?"

He slowly got off the bar stool.

"Or do you want me to hold something else for you?" she shouted after him as he made his way to the back of the room.

He entered the bathroom and his heart sank as he noticed there were no windows. Just wall to wall nudity of women ripped from the pages of 1980's porn magazines tacked to the paneling.

He rinsed his hands in the small rusted sink. There was no soap. He splashed water onto his face and noticed there were no towels in the dispenser either.

He jumped as a meaty sun-burned farm boy slammed the bathroom door open and looked him up and down and then proceeded to pee in the metal trough serving as a urinal. He opened the bathroom door and Mary was leaning on the opposite wall of the small hallway.

"No windows, Mr. Daugherty." she said knowingly.

"What?" he asked nervously.

"Don't tell me you weren't looking for a way to get out of here."

"I need a smoke. Can we go outside and catch some air?"

"Filthy habit, Gerry. There's a smoking area out back."

She nodded to the back door. Hope made a silent cry inside of him. Surely he could outrun her and make it to the car and drive right the fuck out of Dodge.

He opened the back door and beyond was a cement slab surrounded by a tall wooden fence. A ratted blue tarpaulin was nailed to the top as a makeshift roof.

He shook out a Camel and lit it.

"How long do you plan on playing this game, Mary?" He asked.

"You're the one playing games, Mr. Daugherty." she said without emotion.

"How the fuck am I playing games? Jesus! Why are you keeping me here? I've got to be in Rochester in a couple days!"

"Oh, come now. I know how you men think. Picking up some poor woman and her child. Trying to gain favor from her daughter. Offering to buy me drinks. Then what? Hah, Gerry beary?? Then WHAT??"

"What the fuck? Are you fucking insane? I only picked you up because I felt bad for you and your daughter. It's like 180 degrees out here! I only offered to buy you a drink because I felt guilty for being a douche bag to you during the trip!"

"You made your bed, Gerry." she grabbed him by the crotch, "Now you're going to sleep in it. You're definitely going to sleep in it."

"Get your fucking hands off of me!"

She only giggled and handed him his drink.

"So serious. So intense. Drink up, silly."

He gulped the last few swallows of cheap whiskey and Sprite. Puffed the last drag of his cigarette and then threw it on the ground.

"Now what?" He said angrily.

"Now we go in and have a few more drinks, maybe play a game of pool....who knows, Mr. Daugherty, maybe even take you home and ride you dry."

"Jesus Christ, you gross bitch!"

He pulled out his Blackberry, but there was still no signal.

"Son of a b----!" suddenly, the world wobbled.

The ground began to spin and vertigo took hold of his brain.

"Did you have too much to drink, sugar?" He heard Mary's far away voice.

Eventually, the ground found him and pulled him close and the world faded to black.

When Gerry awoke the room was black. Colors swirled in his view and a musty smell mixed with the smell of sex and sweat filled his nostrils.

He tried to rub the sleep from his eyes but his hands weren't cooperating. He tugged at them and realized he was tied to a metal bed frame. The more he tugged at his hands the tighter the nylon rope dug into his wrists.

"What the fuck?" he uttered into the dark room.

He tried to kick his legs and his ankles were tied down too. Next to him, Mary laid naked. Snoring loudly with her back turned to him.

"Oh, Jesus! Oh, fuck!"

His hands and feet wriggled and then he noticed he was naked as well. Mary snorted and he froze as her heavy bare shape rolled over and her arm and heavy leg draped over his shivering body.

"Oh, God, no!" he uttered under his breath.

He took a deep breath and calmed himself. He tried his hands again and then Mary stirred. He tried to stop himself from crying out loud.

Her hand drifted down his chest and stopped on his penis. Her fat little fingers acted like spider's legs and found their way around the shaft and rested there.

"Mary?" he whispered, checking to see if she was awake.

No answer. Her grip neither tightened nor loosened.

He knew he couldn't move without waking her. He decided he'd have to wait until she rolled over again.

When his eyes adjusted to the darkness of the room he scanned around looking for his clothes. He saw his pants lying in a neat pile on top of the dresser by the window.

An hour had passed and she hadn't moved, only lying there with her leg draped over his and his penis in her grip. Her snore rattled in his ear.

He began thinking about what she had done with him. Sickening him and making him feel dirty. Where was Mindy when all this was going on? This place can't be that big? What has that poor girl seen? What has she heard?

Hope visited him again that night when Mary shifted but was smothered when Mary mumbled in her sleep.

"Oh, Gerry beary." she gurgled, and then snuggled even closer to him.

He could feel her naked breasts flopped against him and her pubic hair dug into his hip. Gerry began to weep silently to himself, and he drifted into unconsciousness again.

His eyes flashed opened when he heard the floor creak. He lifted his head and looked towards the doorway but could only see shadows. Mary had released him from her coils and was back on her side again with her back to him.

"This is it." he thought to himself, "I just need one hand free...."

He decided it would be better to concentrate on only one limb, and the lucky winner was his right hand. Focusing completely on the twists and turns of the rope and the angle of his hand he manipulated it lose enough that he felt the slack in his arm.

"I'm so close." he thought, "So goddamn close. Don't wake up, Mary, you fucking bitch! Don't you wake up!"

He jiggled his hand back and forth trying to get the fat part of his hand through the rope.

"Going somewhere, Tiger?" Mary asked from his side.

"Fuck!" he yelled and pulled at his right hand as hard as he could.

Mary rolled over on top of him almost crushing the air from him. He began to panic which made his breathing worse.

"Get off me, you fucking bitch!" he wheezed from his tired lungs, making a quick mental note to quit smoking.

Mary was trying to ram her tongue into his ear as he struggled with his right hand. He could feel her hips beginning to grind into his.

His right wrist felt a raw burn and then it was free. He tried to reach over and undo his left wrist while simultaneously keeping Mary off of him. The latter was fruitless.

"Stay with me, Gerry!" she screamed into his ear as she pulled at his right arm, "Stay with me!!!"

He was beginning to black out from suffocation. He was wheezing, and the only thing in his favor was the sweat between their bodies that kept her from getting a firm grip on him.

But eventually, she found his cock and she grabbed on with such ferocity he thought would rip it right off. He cried out.

"You'll stay with me, Gerry!" she growled, "You'll stay with me and you'll love me! Do you hear me, Gerry! You'll love me!!"

She widened her legs and was beginning to put him inside her when she let out a guttural moan.

He didn't know if it was a moan of pleasure or what. She gripped his penis tighter and then she let out another moan again and let him go.

The ache from his groin was excruciating. Above him, 3 inches from his face was hers. Her beady eyes were wide with a surprised look in them. She jerked and moaned again. Drool leaked from her open mouth and landed on the corner of his lips.

"Mary?" he said feeling her entire body relax on top of his.

Thats when he heard a growl behind Mary and an almost silent CHUNK. Mary squeaked out a breath and then went limp on top of him. Blood leaked out from her mouth and spilled into his face.

Suddenly, he felt the rope tighten on his left hand and then it broke lose. The rope on his left ankle tightened and then it was free and the same with his right.

That's when he realized, Mary was dead. Or dying. Her breathing was shallow and almost non-existent. That same look of shock in her glassy eyes.

He pushed her off and she slid to the floor with a splat. He sat up and saw Mindy standing there with a butcher knife in her trembling hand.

"Mindy?" he said pulling the sheet over his nakedness, "Mindy are you---?"

"Momma." she sobbed not moving, "Maaaaa....maaaaaaa...."

Gerry wrapped the sheet around his waist and found his pants. He slowly slipped them on under the sheet.

"Mindy, honey, it'll be okay....you, did a good thing."

She only stood there with that dripping blade croaking "Maaaaa maaaaaaa" over and over again.

"Come here, Mindy, it's okay." he tried to grab her but she slashed out and cut his forearm.

"Jesus!" he said.

Mary let out a long drawn out moan and Mindy jumped onto her mother's body and began stabbing her repeatedly. Screaming "maaaaaa maaaaaaa" over and over again.

Gerry could still hear her when he got into his car.

It was 10 years later; Gerry was in his prime.

He had written a novel based on his incident with Mary. It was called "Quite Contrary". Published by Penguin 3 years after that fateful road trip in hardcover through two printings. A year later, the paperback exploded off the shelves and he sold the movie rights to Project Greenlight.

The book itself exaggerated itself with gory details and added in maybe a few heroic moves by the protagonist of the story. The names were changed, all except for Mary's. Hollywood added their own touch to further ticket sales. It worked, but by the end of it all, much of the truth of the story was lost in fiction and pizazz.

Gerry was dealing with it well though. Quite well. After the movie was released, his book went back into reprint and he went on another tour with the book. He still drove it. But stayed off the back roads. He could taste bile in the back of his throat every time he drove past a hitchhiker.

Today, he was back in Rochester, MN. Barnes and Noble booksellers signing a long line of paperback editions of "Quite Contrary". He even signed a few movie posters and 8 x 10 photos. He had done plenty of public readings and went over the story in several interviews that he had lost sight of what had really happened along that long stretch of road in southern Minnesota.

Thirty-eight people were turned away at 8:30pm. He had had enough of the glitz and fandom and just wanted to hop in his car and take a ride to his hotel in Minneapolis. He thanked the crowd and apologized, reminding them that they could see him at the Mall of America tomorrow from 2pm to 7pm.

"You're headed right for your hotel?" Ronnie is manager asked.

"Yeah, yeah." Gerry answered perturbed.

"There's a bar at the hotel, you know, Ger."

"Jesus fuck, Ronnie! I get it! I'll get back to my hotel like a good little doggie!"

"You don't need to be a prick, Gerry, I'm only looking out for your safety."

"You know what? I had a mother for 42 years. She died. I don't need a mother anymore at 52."

"Do you want me to have them get your car for you?"

"I'm your top money maker, Ronnie, not your goddamn son! Nobody touches or drives my fuckin' car. You know that. I'll see you tomorrow."

With that, he left. His full intention was to go straight to the hotel in Minneapolis, but now that his agent was being a prick he wanted to stop off at the bar on the way. Hell, maybe even two bars; just to show that sonofabitch who he was talking to.

In the parking ramp he reached his old '68. He popped the trunk and put in his briefcase. He slammed it down and then realized someone was behind him.

"Mr. Daugherty?" said a female voice.

He froze in his tracks and to be honest, he almost lost the contents of his bladder. The voice was very familiar. It was Mary's. He was sure of it. He would never forget the gravelly toothless lisp of that grotesque glob of a woman.

"You still drivin' that old car, Mr. Daughterty?" she said again.

He let out a breath, "Muh...Mary?"

"Turn around, let me get a look atchoo."

He turned around. But the large grotesque shape wasn't there. The fat doughy face was thin, and the body had turned into a series of well-placed curves.

"Min...dy?" he uttered in disbelief.

"Hey, Mr. Daugherty." she said with a half-smile, "You do remember me."

"Remember you? My, God, how have you been? I.....I'm so sorry, Mindy. So sorry about what happened with your mom."

"That was a long time ago. You weren't the first person she did that to. There were many others before you...."

"Before me? My God, how...how many?"

"I lost count after the first ten. Every one she ended up tellin' the boys downstairs that her man put his hands on me and the boys would take the guy out and kill him. Cut him up and throw him to the pigs."

"Oh, Jesus..."

"Pigs eat anything and everything, Mr. Daugherty. Well, 'cept the skull. Can't fit it into their mouths. So, you gotta break that up with a hammer."

"You poor dear. The things you must have..."

Mindy put her hand up to interrupt him, "I didn't come here for your sympathy, Mr. Daugherty."

"But...but...I left you." the realization of what he did upset him, "I left you after you killed your own mother."

"Like I said, Mr. Daugherty, that was a long time ago. I came here to get what's due to me."

"Uh....excuse me?"

"I saved your life, Mr. Daugherty. But that's not what I mean, human beings are supposed to help each other when in dire need."

"Then...what?"

"You made a lot of money offa my story. Most of which didn't even happen. You took a lot of liberties with it."

"It's a novel, Mindy. The only people who knew the truth behind the story is you, me and your mom."

"The movie took a lot more liberties with my story. I didn't really like that actress that played me either...."

"So...you want money?"

"Me and the boys think we deserve a lot more than money for what you wrote about us."

"The boys?"

From dark recesses of the parking ramp, a few familiar faces appeared from the shadows. They were some of the men from "The Legend".

"I don't understand what you mean, Mindy? If you want money I can get you..."

"Keep your money, Mr. Daugherty. I got plenty when mama died. But you do owe me your life. I saved yours and you took mine away."

"What? Took it..."

"Shut the fuck up, Mr. Daugherty. You left me holding a knife crying over my dead mama. What sort of a man does that? I was left with these men to raise me. We got rid of mama's body the way we always git rid of bodies. I was raised in that bar by these men. When I was old enough, they put themselves in me. I got pregnant by Frank over there. But miscarried..."

"I'm so..."

"You owe me your life, Mr. Daugherty, and I aim to take it."

The boys from the bar surrounded him and he felt a sharp blow to the back of his head and after the stars twinkled in his head, he faded into blackness.

When his lights turned on again, he was back in Enderson Grove. On the outskirts, at least. The scent of manure and that yeasty scent of silage stung his nose. He saw that he was strapped to a metal cow panel. His pants were missing as were his underwear. His penis hung in the cool night air.

"What the fuck is this??" he screamed.

Mindy came from an adjoining pen. Behind her, the boys of the Legend were leading a small calf that was bucking and crying out. They held it tight with a rope.

"Redemption." Mindy said in a low cold voice.

"C'mon, Mindy, you don't have to do this! People are going to be looking for me!"

"You mean that manager that you treat like shit? The boys took care of him. He's in the pig pen over there. Should be about gone in an hour."

"Ronnie?"

"You'll be in there soon, Mr. Daugherty. But not until you die a deserving death."

"Please, Mindy..." he was beginning to cry.

"Do you know what happens when you starve a calf?" she says trying to pet the restless beast the men were holding, "When you introduce something into their mouths they begin to suck at it. Powerfully. They suck until they can get their mother's milk."

She walked up to Gerry and grabbed his dick, "How much mother's milk do you think this young starving calf will get from this, Mr. Daugherty?"

"No! No! Noooo! NO! NOOO! Please, Mindy!" he tried to wriggle from his bonds as the calf was led closer and closer.

LIGHTS IN THE SKY

On April 30th, 2009, I was flying a kite with my youngest daughter. While we enjoyed the perfect kite-flying weather, I spotted 6 U.F.O.s in a V-formation flying south to north. Much of the beginning of this story really happened. The rest was fiction.

Wind is best harvested in late April on the southern plains of Minnesota. It's when the windsurfers hit the lakes in their wetsuits after being cooped up for the 5 months of winter weather. It's when the wind turbines are at their peak electricity production. It's also one of the best times to fly a kite.

The day was overcast, the sky a transparent blue layered with light puffy clouds. The wind blew at 35 mph from the south; A welcome warm breeze from the former frigid air.

Out on the Fair Lakes Soccer Fields, two lone figures stand. One, short in stature, is an 8-year-old girl. The other is a 38-year-old male who is obviously her father. Together they are attempting to tame the wind with a kite he had purchased earlier that day.

The young girl, giddy with anticipation to pilot the kite, is grabbing with little hands to hold the string. The man places the roll of high gauge white string in her welcoming hands while he backs up with the kite.

Already the wind wants it, rippling the wings and fluttering the three stripped plastic tail. When he reaches a distance of about 50 feet from his daughter he stops.

"Are you ready, honey?" he shouts.

"Yeah!" her heart thumping in her chest "let it go! Let it go!"

"Hold tight!"

"I will, daddy, let it go!"

He let it go, and like a rocket it zipped into the air with ferocious speed. His daughter squealed with delight that melted his heart.

"Keep the string tight!" he instructed as he ran up to her.

"I will, daddy, *gosh*!" she frowned at him causing him to laugh.

To his surprise she took to it like a natural. The kite zipped and dived until she had the string tight enough it just steadily raised itself into the sky.

"Perfect, Lisa!" he says, "Good job!"

She stood silently with a perma-smile on her lips.

"Gonna need braces for that one." he thinks to himself, *"Better start saving now!"*

"Can I make it go higher, daddy?" she asks innocently.

"Sure!" he agrees, "Just keep that string tight!"

"Quit saying that!"

He will remember how blue her eyes are, like a perfect reflection of the sky. He will remember that crooked-toothed smile with the little gap in between the front two teeth. He will never forget, no matter how many whiskeys he drinks, the next few moments either.

He knelt behind her trying to get an artsy shot with his flip phone. He looked off into the sky to the south. There were geese and planes and insects zipping their way across the sky. But something else caught his eye.

There were six objects flying in a "V" formation from the south heading north. At first he thought they were geese, as that was their normal flying pattern. But as they got closer he noticed they were too large to be geese. He next deduced that they were probably aircraft; there was an air force base in nearby Sioux City, Iowa.

But they didn't make a sound. As they flew overhead he thought they were spherical in shape. He tried to register this and couldn't take his eyes off of them.

"I'm not seeing this right." He thought to himself, *"What the hell kind of aircraft is spherical?"*

The objects were hundreds of feet beyond the kite now, rapidly making their way north.

"Honey," he asked Lisa. "Do you see that?"

"What, daddy?" she asked not taking her eye off the kite.

"Those shapes up there in the sky. Above your kite?"

"What shapes? Those clouds?"

"Look, just above them." he said trying to aim her gaze with his finger.

Just as she caught sight of them, they disengaged from their flight pattern and zipped in impossible angles from each other as if they were dancing in the sky.

"What the---??" Lisa said letting go of her kite.

With that they all dove into a cloud.

"You saw it?" he asked frantically.

"Daddy, my kite!" she went running for the undulating roll of string.

"But you saw it, didn't you?"

"I don't know. It was weird."

"Oh my god, Lisa! I think we just saw a group of U.F.O.'s!"

"Daddy! My kite is flying away!"

He looked at the cloud those objects had dove into and then ran after the kite. Lisa screamed in support of his chase. He was getting winded and cursed ever starting up smoking.

He leaped at the roll of kite string that got caught on a lump of grass and had hold of it. The chaos of the kite's flight pattern made the kite string rub against his face giving him a burn.

"Goddammit!" he cursed beneath his breath.

He pulled it tight and began to wind the kite up. He was backing his way back to Lisa.

"There you go, honey." He said still staring up at the sky, watching for more of those things.

"Honey? Here take the kite."

He looked down and noticed his daughter wasn't there.

"Lisa?" he looked behind him. She wasn't there. He spun in every direction but she wasn't anywhere to be seen. The entire soccer fields were empty; it was just him.

He ran to his Toyota, but she wasn't there either.

"Lisa!!" he shouted, but was only answered by the wind.

He ran to the little brick building that housed the concessions and bathrooms. The doors were locked tight, but he still pounded on them shouting her name.

He pulled out his phone and dialed 9-1-1.

"nine one one emergency, state the nature of your call, please"

"I need to…." He didn't know how to word it, "I need to report a missing child."

"Can I get your name, sir, and a description of the child missing?"

"My name. My name is Daniel Sutter. I am the girl's father. Her name is Lisa Anne Sutter. She is 8 years old. Brunette with blue eyes."

"Are you calling from a mobile phone, sir?"

"Yes. I'm at the soccer fields."

"We are sending an officer to your location. Can you please stay on the line and answer a few more questions, please?"

"I can't…I have to…find her!"

"I understand that, sir, but the more information we have, the better we can…"

Dan hung up the phone and started to weep. He didn't know what he was going to tell his wife.

2.

"Do you have any idea how ridiculous you sound?" Margret screamed into his face, "Do you??"

Dan bowed his head, his eyes stung from crying for the last hour.

"I know how it sounds!" he defended. "You think I don't know how crazy it sounds?? Jesus, I was right there! Lisa was right there!"

Detective Bueller wrote in his notebook.

"You're sure there was no one else on the soccer fields with you?" Bueller asked, "I mean, it's a big complex, you didn't see any other vehicles parked there besides your own?"

"No." Dan answered, "I'm sure of it."

Bueller looked at Margret, "We have officers and volunteers canvassing the neighborhood since we released the amber alert for Lisa."

"Thank you." She began to sob again.

"You didn't get any reports about…about…." Dan didn't know how to word it, "…things in the sky?"

"Shut up about that, goddammit!!" Margret punched him in the arm, "Our daughter is missing and you're worried about aliens??"

"I think they're the ones that took her." He said reluctantly.

Margret began to pummel him until Det. Bueller stepped in and pulled her off of him.

"You're not going to find your daughter this way, Mrs. Sutter."

He said calmly.

Bueller sat Margret down on a chair away from the couch they were sitting on and then looked at Dan.

"In answer to your question, Mr. Sutter, no. We've spoke with the air force base, the local airport and with the FAA. There have been no….anomalies reported today."

"I don't….understand…how…?" Dan was speaking more to himself than anyone else.

"You need to go and search for our daughter, Daniel!" Margret spat, "You're sitting here on the couch babbling like a madman about science fiction while some maniac has our child!"

Dan stood up to go out, but Bueller stopped him.

"Actually, Margret," Detective Bueller interrupted. "I'll need to talk with Dan at the station."

"What??" Margret said surprised.

"Am I under arrest?" Dan asked distantly, his mind was still playing back what he had seen.

"No." Bueller answered, "Just have a few more questions for you. I'd appreciate it if you would ride along with me."

"I don't really have a choice do I?"

"I'm being polite, Mr. Sutter."

"You think he did it, don't you?" Margret spoke up in horror, "That makes sense! It all makes sense! You probably killed her, didn't you?"

"Marge, no!" Dan answered hurt, "How could you…?"

"You were always so jealous since she was born. Always whining about how I paid more attention to her than I did you!"

"Jesus, what are you doing?"

"Yeah, it all makes sense now! Do you remember when I found that pornography you were looking at online? Deviant! You sick son-of-a-bitch! You probably did God knows what to her and then killed her! I want you out! I want you----!"

"Okay, that's enough!" Bueller was getting upset, "You're not helping anything, Mrs. Sutter. Now back off and let us leave without any incident."

Dan began to sob even harder in disbelief that his wife of 15 years had turned on him. Bueller led him out to the back of his car, Margret still screaming at him from inside the house.

They had arrived at the Moon Valley County Security Building. The Fair Lake Police station was downstairs, the Sheriff's offices were on the main floor, and the jail and dispatch area were on the top floor.

They drove into a security garage and they opened the back door of the car when the garage door was secure. They led Dan down a cream colored hallway to an empty sterile looking conference room.

"Have a seat." Bueller said, "Can I get you a coffee or anything?"

Dan shook his head and Bueller decided to get him one anyways and left him alone in the room locking the door behind him.

"Who do you got?" Detective Williams another detective for Fair Lake asked him in the hall.

"Dan Sutter." Bueller answered, "His daughter turned up missing when they were allegedly flying a kite out at the soccer fields."

"You think he had something to do with it?"

"The guy is claiming U.F.O.'s took his daughter, so what do you think?"

"Any priors on the guy?"

"None. The guy is squeaky clean. Not even a speeding or parking ticket. That's the only reason I haven't officially arrested him."

"Gonna do a psych eval on him?"

"Maybe, I'll see what turns up after the inter----"

The lights flickered, then went off completely for two seconds and then came back on.

"Looks like the mayor didn't pay the light bill again." Williams joked and then walked back down the hall to his own office.

Bueller maneuvered two full cups of coffee down the hall the opposite way to the door with only spilling a small amount on his hands. Luckily, he didn't burn himself.

"Mr. Sutter, I----" Bueller stood there staring into an empty room with his mouth open.

"Mr. Sutter?"

The room was completely empty.

"Shit!" he pulled out his radio that was on his hip, "Dispatch, I want all the doors locked down. No one gets out! I need every available unit inside the station to be on the lookout for a white male, 38, black hair with a slight beard. He was wearing a dark blue t-shirt and faded jeans. Hold him and let me know if you find him. Bueller, out."

An hour search turned up nothing. Bueller had the files from the security camera in the conference room sent to his laptop. Williams came over to his desk and watched the tape with him.

The file shows Dan sitting at a table. His head slumped and his face in his hands. It looks as if he is crying. Then some sort of interference obscures the picture for a brief moment.

"What the fuck is that?" Bueller mutters.

"What?" Williams squints at the screen.

"That right there."

There are a few items on the table that seem to be shaking as if the table were vibrating. Dan is looking at the table dumbfounded.

"What the hell is going on?" Williams squint turns into a grimace.

Just then, the image of Dan and the items that were on the table are actually floating in midair, just above the table. The screen distorts again, and he is gone along with the items that were on the table.

"Shit!" Bueller said.

"Kevin," Williams started. "What the fuck was that?"

Kevin didn't answer. He just breathed heavily through his nose staring at the paused screen shot.

"Kevin?" Williams shook his shoulder lightly, "C'mon, you with me, man?"

"We're going to have to erase this file." He said finally.

"What? Erase it? Are you fucking kidding me? We can't erase it, this is evidence!"

"Evidence of what?" He looked at Williams coldly.

"Well…this….I don't know! But…it's…Jesus, man!"

"We can say we tried to review the file but it was glitched up and when we tried to clean it up we accidently erased it."

"Kevin….that's…"

"That's the truth."

Williams was quiet for a moment and then said, "It still doesn't explain away where he went to?"

"He escaped. It's that simple. We'll catch hell for incompetence, but it's a lot fuckin' easier to explain that than what we just saw on that video!"

3. *Two Years Later*

It was Anne Silvers first flight as captain. Her Boeing 787 was on a return flight from Belize to Ft. Lauderdale, Florida. She would admit later that 'yes', she did indeed have a drink before her flight.

"It was just a quick nip off a travel flask." She said to the FAA board and her superiors at South Am Airways, "I was nervous about my first flight as captain."

There was no turbulence that day, low clouds, but no storm systems for the flight. As far as maiden flights go, today was perfect.

"We're just above Mexico City, captain." Her first officer said.

"Thanks, Mel." She smiled back.

They had leveled off at 35,000 feet and engaged the auto-pilot.

"How does the weather look?" she asked her flight engineer.

"There is a storm front but it's out of our flight path to the northwest." He said, "Otherwise it's clear sa------"

"Something wrong, Eddie?"

"I'm getting something odd on the radar scope. It's not clear, but it's not...normal."

Anne got up and looked at what he was seeing. She had him set the scope at 28 nautical miles range. There were several objects 11.6 miles in the 7 o'clock position that was heading in the same direction they were in.

"What the hell?" she muttered.

"Uh...captain?" Mel said from the co-pilot seat, "You might want to see this."

She sat back into her chair and noticed a faint vibration thrum through the plane. It began to get more and more intense.

"Look at the altitude meter." He said.

It began spinning up then down in some erratic pattern.

"What the hell?" she said again.

Just then, the engines cut off. The vibration on the plane got so bad she thought her teeth would rattle out of her head. The thrum was inside her head and judging by the reaction of her crew, they felt/heard it too.

There was nothing but a brilliant light outside the cockpit windows. She didn't know if they were falling or moving forward or just standing still.

Just before she thought the vibration would rattle her body apart, the engines kicked in again. The thrum was gone and the sky was clear again.

They all looked dazed. Eddie felt something foreign in his mouth and then spit it out onto his hand. It was a filling from his right side molar.

Anne looked at the instrument panel and everything was reading normal.

"Captain?" it was the intercom between the flight crew and the service crew.

"Go ahead, Adam." Anne said.

"I think you need to come back here if you can."

She remembered in her training that under a hijack situation, there was a code they were to give if there was something like that happening on board.

"Code 27?" she asked.

"No. I'm not sure how to explain this."

Anne knew there was an air marshal on board so she felt a little at ease. She grabbed the .38 from the gun locker just in case.

"Keep us level." She said to Mel, "And try to get ahold of the nearest ATC. Find out if they've seen anything."

"Be careful." Eddie said as she left the cockpit.

As she walked out into the cabin, most of the first class passengers were asleep. Those that weren't looked a bit scared and dazed. The first class stewardess motioned for her to come back into business class.

"What is going on? What just happened?" a passenger had asked.

"We're trying to assess the situation and when I have a clear answer I'll let everyone know." She answered, "As for now, the plane is safe, we're still on course, and all equipment is running normal."

She made her way into Business class and heard a man yelling from the lavatory. There were several people, mostly men, gathered behind Adam the head steward.

"Adam," she said behind the crowd. "What's going on?"

Crouched in the fetal position, was a naked man. He was Caucasian, but his skin was a dark pink like he suffered 3rd degree burns. Steam drifted off of his wet black hair and his eyes were wide with fear.

"Adam?" she asked her steward again.

"He...he just..." Adam thought for a moment, "He just appeared here out of nowhere."

"What??"

"I know how it sounds. Believe me. But before whatever happened outside the craft, there was no one inside either lavatory. Then after...all that...I hear this screaming from inside this one and I opened the door and found him lying there....like...like this."

The man was no longer screaming, he was only muttering to himself.

"Does he have any family on board?" Anne asked.

"As far as I can see...he's not even supposed to be on this flight."

"What the hell are you saying?"

"He's not supposed to be on this flight. South Am overbooked us, so we're full. Every person who has a ticket is present and accounted for except him."

Anne licked her lips, they were getting dry. She rubbed her forehead and tried to reason.

"Maybe he stowed away?" Anne said.

"The hatch to the storage area is locked from this side." Adam said putting a blanket over the man.

Anne knelt down next to him, "What's your name, sir?"

The man shivered and winced at the sound of her voice.

"You're safe now. I need your name so I can contact your family."

He looked at her from the corner of his eyes.

"Do you speak English?"

"My...my...family?" he uttered.

"Yes, sir, what's your name?"

"Luh...lee....Lisa?"

"Your name is...Lisa?"

He frowned and then looked up at her.

"My daughter. Lisa. Where is she? I had her...I had her right here in my arms!"

"It was just you, sir." Adam said, "It was just you I found in the lavatory."

"Where am I?"

"You're on South Am flight 210 from Belize to Ft. Lauderdale." Anne said.

The man looked around as if the words sounded foreign to him.

"I'm on a plane?" panic flashed in his eyes, "Get me down! Get me down! Please, God, get me down. I don't want to be up here! Not up in the air with those things all around! Please get me down."

"Calm down, sir." Anne had her hand on the grip of the revolver, "We're here to help you."

"You don't understand! I cannot be up here! I can't do it!"

Someone came up the aisle with a prescription bottle. A woman about 39 years old, good looking, and perhaps famous.

"Here." She said, "This will knock him out."

"No!" he protested, "Get me out of the sky! Get me out of the sky!!"

Some of the passengers who were gathered around them helped pin him down and they got the pills down his throat.

Within a long 20 minutes, he was out.

Despite the amount of witnesses to former captain Anne Silvers testimony. She was grounded, and would not captain a flight for South Am Airways again.

4.

Detective Kevin Bueller was eating at his favorite spot. Eddie's

Café off 1st and Main. It had been a staple of downtown Fair Lakes since the depression. Owned by the same family since and the menu hadn't changed like the rest of the health conscious world.

Before him sat a blazing yellow order of hash browns, two links of sausage and a mash of scrambled eggs. He was finishing his toast when his cell phone went off.

"Yeah?" he said.

"Bueller," it was dispatch. "I have a phone call from the U.S. Marshal's office in Ft. Lauderdale. I think you may want to take this."

"Send it through."

There was a double beep and then, "Detective Bueller?"

"Yes, can I help you?"

"Sgt. Acosta with the U.S. Marshal's office."

"Good morning, Sgt., to what do I owe this honor?"

"Do you know a person named Daniel Levi Sutter? Age 41? Caucasian, black hair, about 6 foot 1?"

Kevin's stomach got sour, but he managed to swallow the eggs in his mouth.

"Detective Bueller?"

"Yes, why?"

"I have him sitting in a holding cell here in Ft. Lauderdale. After we printed him we got a hit in the database that your agency was looking for him."

"Where did you pick him up?"

"That's a whole story in itself. But the just of it is he was found on a plane coming from Belize to here. He caused quite an uproar on board; not to mention he was naked during all this. He was subdued by the passengers and an air marshal and tranquilized. He was handed over to me and now I'm calling you."

"Has he said anything?"

"Yeah. The guy's a nutcase. Keeps claiming he was abducted by a U.F.O. That's why he panicked on the plane, said he didn't want to be in the air with…'those things' as he put it.

"According to his file he's wanted for the murder of his daughter?"

"Abduction, we haven't found a body yet."

"Well, he claimed that his daughter…Lisa…was on this spacecraft with him and that these…things…were going to let them go but only let him go."

Bueller only grunted a response.

"Well, other than being completely batshit," Acosta said. "I don't really have any charges on him."

"I'll put through paperwork to have the D.O.C. expedite him here; that is, if you don't mind holding him until then?"

"No problem, Detective."

"Thank you, Sgt."

"The guy is a bit of an escape artist, so perhaps I should have him confined to maximum security?"

I'm not sure that would help. He thought to himself, *If they want him, they'll just take him.*

"Whatever you think is best." He said instead.

5.

Dan Sutter sat with his eyes wide and blood-shot. He looked tan but his skin was peeling like from a bad sunburn. Kevin remembered that the man had thick black curly hair which was thin now, patchy, and straight with streaks of dead white in it.

He was muttering almost inaudible whispers to himself which Kevin was straining to hear.

"Did you call his wife?" one of the officers in the observation room asked.

"Nope." Detective Bueller said, "I want to talk to him before anyone gets notified."

"Okay. The guy looks like shit."

Kevin only looked at the officer and then asked him to turn off the camera as he walked out of the dark room into the conference room.

"You look like you need a smoke." Bueller said as he walked into the room.

Dan jumped but only shook his head.

"Do you want me to notify your wife?"

"No." he said quietly as Kevin sat down.

"Why don't we start where you and I left off?"

"I don't remember."

"How do you not remember a thing like that? I watched the tape, Mr. Sutter, I can't explain what I saw but goddammit it haunts my dreams."

"You saw what happened?"

"You disappeared. Right before my eyes. BANG ZAP! Just like that!"

"So you believe me then?"

"I'm not sure what I believe, but you need to tell me what happened to you after you….left here."

"I've been trying. It's foggy."

"Why don't you start with what happened the day you disappeared?" Kevin said lighting a Marlboro from a dying pack.

Everywhere in Minnesota was smoke free, but he didn't care at this point. Because he really didn't know if he wanted to hear this man's story. He only knew he had to find this man's daughter.

"They took me."

"Who took you?"

Dan looked up at the florescent lights, "Them."

"Aliens, Mr. Sutter?"

"Yuh..yuh…yess."

"The same ones you claimed two years ago took your daughter Lisa?"

"Lisa? Yes, oh my God, Lisa! They were letting us go! They were letting us go but they kept her!"

Dan began to sob.

"Get ahold of yourself, Mr. Sutter. I can't help you unless you pull yourself together and start talking sense."

"Do you believe in God, detective?"

"I...I guess. I'm not a church goer, but I guess I believe in something up---"

"There is no God, detective."

Kevin crushed out his cigarette and pulled the second to the last one out and lit it.

"You see what I've seen, detective, and you realize this. I was raised a strict Catholic. I taught Sunday school, went to men's bible study, went to confession more times than days I've been alive.

"All of that went to shit on that day."

Kevin looked down at his arm and the hairs were standing on end. He rubbed his arm and let Dan continue his story.

"I don't remember what happened after you left me in this room, detective. I only remember feeling like my skeleton was going to vibrate out of my skin and then everything went black.

"When I came to, I was...I was in this...this cocoon type thing. It was like...like skin. Then it filled with some sort of jelly type of thing that numbed my entire body. I was paralyzed. I couldn't see through the gel and the sounds were muffled outside my cocoon. I was vaguely aware that they were pulling on my body."

Dan motioned to the pack of cigarettes. There was only one left, Kevin didn't want to give it up, but he nodded. He pulled out the last smoke and lit it for him. Dan choked in deep coughs and then settled holding the cigarette tight in his lips.

After he had a few puffs from it, Kevin put it out for him.

"They opened up the cocoon where my head was….oh my God! I thought I was going to go mad when I saw them! Oh, Jesus Christ!"

"What did they look like?"

"They sure as hell didn't look like Chewabacca or Yoda!! They were grey….no mouths…which in a way relieved me…because if they didn't have mouths…they couldn't eat me…"

"Eat you?"

"I know…it sounds crazy. But that's what was going through my head. They had enormous heads that sat impossibly on long thick necks…..their eyes…oh God their eyes! They were…black….like it was two large almond shaped pupils looking at you!

"I was begging for them to just kill me. I could feel myself go insane, like my…my normal self just let go and disappeared so I started to laugh. I laughed so loud that I think I scared them a little bit. That's when they brought in Lisa."

Dan started to cry again. Snot and tears hung off his face.

"I'm going to get some tissue for you, Mr. Sutter." Kevin said getting up. He looked at the ceiling and then said, "I'll be right back, don't lose your train of thought."

6.

Kevin had grabbed a box of kleenix from his desk drawer. Next to it was a silver flask of Bushmills. He looked around, it was shift change so there was no one around the office. He took three quick nips off the flask and then went to his partner's desk. Slid open the bottom drawer and took a fresh pack of cigs from a carton and then dropped a $5 bill inside.

He stood outside the door wondering what he would find when he opened it. He took a deep whiskey scented breath, and then walked inside.

After he had another smoke and cleaned up his face; Dan sat reluctantly in his chair as if he were hanging above a deep cliff.

"So." Kevin said, "Lisa?"

"Yes." Dan's eyes began to water, "She was inside a smaller cocoon. She was also covered in the jelly; her eyes were wide open, but I don't think she could see me."

Tears streamed impossibly down Dan's face as if he were a statuary fountain.

"They let me hold her." He continued, "I got to hold her for about two minutes and then they pried her from my grasp. I was just holding this cocoon, but I knew she was alive.

"I was sealed back up into my own cocoon and I blacked out."

"Did they communicate with you at all?" Kevin said trying not to sound like a nut job.

"Have you ever read the Bible, detective?" Dan asked.

"Uh…sure, I guess."

"No. I mean *really* read the Bible."

"I thought you said you don't believe in God?"

"That has nothing to do with this. The bible is a historical record. There have been archeological findings to prove certain facts written in the bible."

"Okay? So what does all of this have to do with....what's going on?"

"Because, detective, they created us. They're God. All the angels, fallen and blessed...they're the ones our ancestors wrote of. The Norse and Greek gods of Olympus, all of them...Native American gods...they're all these things!"

Kevin opened his mouth and then closed it again.

"They've been manipulating us genetically for eons! Don't you get it? We're all just some lab experiment!"

The guy had lost his marbles. Despite what Kevin had seen, he knew that Dan Sutter's mind was a snakepit of insanity.

"When you....went missing..." Kevin said. "I told my superiors that you had escaped somehow. I risked my job."

"Why?"

"Because I believe you....somewhat. I don't think you kidnapped your daughter."

"But you don't believe that THEY took me?"

"How did you end up on the plane?"

Dan had lit another cigarette. He coughed for about 5 minutes straight and spat something red and black into the trash can.

"They put me there." Dan said slowly between gasps.

"They...they...teleported you there?"

"I guess....it was...the...same tech...technology that took me."

Another coughing fit and Kevin thought he would need to call a paramedic this time.

"Why do you think they kept your daughter?"

Dan wept again with another furious bout of coughing. When he stopped his lungs were wheezing.

"They didn't…I…I don't think.…I don't think she survived the teleportation."

Kevin poured him a glass of ice water which he greedily gulped.

"The teleportation…it.…it weakens the flesh.…"

Dan fell to the ground and curled into the fetal position coughing again.

"Jesus, man, are you okay?" Kevin asked.

"Look at the stars, detective. Look at the stars."

With that bit of advice, Dan Sutter's body disintegrated into a puddle of clear liquid.

7.

Detective Kevin Sutter was asked to retire early. He had three years left till pension, but he also had several months of personal time saved up. So he retired early and he was asked to keep his mouth shut about aliens and never to mention Daniel Sutter again.

He moved to a cabin on Leech Lake in northern Minnesota. He spends his time fishing and hunting alone. Every deer season his nephew joins him at the cabin.

He and his nephew are staring up at the clear night sky. It is flooded with stars. A meteor shower is supposed to appear in the northern sky. Uncle Kevvy points out the different constellations to his nephew. As he names each one he thinks about their origins, names of the Greek gods and goddesses; and he thinks about what Mr. Sutter told him in that cold interrogation room:

"Because, detective, they created us. They're God"

"What's that one, Uncle Kevin?" his nephew asks.

"Which one?" Kevin squints.

"That one, next to Orion's Belt?"

It was a strange pattern he had never seen before. He pulled out his binoculars to get a better look. That's when the pattern broke apart and zig zagged across the night sky.

"What was *that*??" his nephew gasped.

"That was....nothing."

Kevin's stomach turned sour as it always does when he felt afraid. 24 years of being a cop had taught him how to smother the fear, but this is what happens when it's been hidden for so long.

"Nothing?? But it...it broke apart and then they...flew..."

He was so scared now that he thought he would either puke or wet his pants.

"C'mon, kiddo, let's go in."

"No way! I know what I saw!"

"It's the meteor shower, that's all it is."

Kevin couldn't help but feel the gooseflesh pop out on his arms.

"Well, I'm staying out here. I don't want to miss this. You can't see this stuff in the city."

"Suit yourself." Kevin went to pull a beer out of the cooler that sat next to his bench on the porch. He wiped the sweaty bottle with a towel he designated as the official bottle/can wiper.

His back was to his nephew. "You want a pop?"

Silence.

LUCIFER'S PARADE

When I was a kid I used to have a lot of nightmares about the end of the world. I still do from time to time, this one was in my 20s. It is a well-known fact that there is a witches coven that runs the downtown Omaha area....

I am writing this on an old corona typewriter. I am somewhere off the interstate just southwest of Omaha, Nebraska in an old abandoned warehouse office.

I write it out of posterity more than anything else. I am a writer, after all, but I don't think I will be publishing anymore novels. I am only holding out in this place for the night and then I'm moving on west or north. I haven't decided which. I saw this typewriter here and decided to write witness to the events that led up to the possible extinction of the human race.

I don't think anyone will read this. Nobody human at least. So this is more or less cathartic.

A few days ago, my wife Stella(RIP) and I decided to take a road trip from our home in Beaverton, Oregon to Omaha, Nebraska to visit an old college friend of mine.

Joey Gnucci owned his own painting business in Omaha. He was very successful with it. He was an economics major in college, but ran his own painting business to live on; so go figure.

When driving to Omaha on Interstate 80 from the west, it comes at you by surprise. Corn. Corn. Corn. Corn. Corn. Corn. BAM! Omaha.

All traffic was detoured around downtown Omaha. It was a standstill on the smaller roads but luckily I knew a few detours of my own to get to his neighborhood and made it back into Omaha proper in fifteen minutes.

The Gnucci's were a well-to-do family with restaurants, jewelry stores, and a couple hotels. Joey inherited his mother's house in a gated community called "The Regency".

When we got to the gate, a security guard stopped us. He checked my license and asked me how I got into Omaha through the detours. I joked that I was once the mayor of Omaha but he didn't find that funny. He made a phone call, I thought to Joey but found out later it was to someone else.

He lifted the gate and we went in.

Joey greeted us and helped us unload the luggage from the trunk. He also asked about how I made it through the detours and he laughed at my mayor joke.

He fed us a typical Italian dinner, baked ziti with bread and clam sauce. The guy was a natural cook. After a few glasses of wine I asked him what was going on in Omaha that they needed to detour traffic out of the city.

I noticed a mood change on his face.

"A parade." He said, "Since you left they started having a parade every year to commemorate some···pagan festival. Solstice maybe."

"Solstice?" I said, "That's not until--- "

"I don't know what it's called, man." He interrupted me, "Anyways, I have to go downtown and finish up a job at a salon."

"But we just got here." My wife Stella said.

"I'm sorry." And he genuinely looked sorry. Almost

too sorry, "But the salon needs to be done before tomorrow morning when they open. "

I offered to help.

"No. " he said almost curtly, "You should just stick around here. I wouldn' t go downtown. It' s too crowded and packed. "

"Uh···okay. I guess we' ll just stick around here until you get back. " I said.

He patted me on the shoulder and then his cell phone rang. He looked at the caller ID and then dismissed himself out of the room.

An hour after he left, we sat out on his patio, enjoying more wine than we really should have. I' ll savor that moment, because it was the last really good time I spent with Stella.

His house sat on top of a bluff that overlooked the city lights of Omaha. Joey was right; it looked very packed with traffic.

"What' s that?" Stella said with her head against my chest.

There was something, almost as tall as the Mutual of Omaha building that I had never noticed before. There were spotlights all around it.

"We should go check it out." She said.

"I don' t know, honey. You know me and crowds." I really hated crowds. Any more than 5 people in a room and I freak out.

But my wife has a way of making me do things I would normally never do, and be comfortable with doing them. Whether it' s those damn brown eyes of hers or those long legs I' ll never know. I just found myself behind the wheel of our Subaru Outback and heading to the front gate of "the Regency".

The gate didn' t open. I honked the horn and the security guard came over to my window.

"Is there a problem?" I asked.

"Where are you going?" he asked.

I looked at Stella and then back at him and laughed.

"What? Are you kidding me?"

"Standard procedure, sir."

I looked at his eyes, and he wasn't kidding. He meant business, and I thought if I refused this man, there would be a fight.

"Just heading to the store to get some more booze!" I said in my best drunk voice I could.

"You really shouldn't be driving if you've been drinking, sir."

"You really shouldn't be harassing me either! My tax dollars are paying your salary, mister!"

Stella tried to conceal a laugh.

"Actually, 'the Regency' association pays my salary, sir."

"Whatever. C'mon, let me and my wife get outta here, I'm thirsty!!"

The guard walked back to his little shack and called someone. When he got off the phone he hit the button to the gate.

"What the fuck was that?" I asked.

"I don't know." Stella said.

"I'm gonna talk to Joe about that shit. Wow!"

So we decided to take a cruise downtown to the old warehouse district. It was a favorite hotspot when I was in college and it has been renovated since then to open Omaha up as a convention center mecca. So I was excited to see how it all turned out.

The warehouse district was insane. It was decorated like it was the holidays. Banners and streamers everywhere, street merchants, musicians and oceans of people. The flags and banners were written in what looked like runes or some ancient celtic writing.

We drove around for about 45 minutes trying to find a parking spot but didn't have any luck. The streets were flooded with traffic both automotive and pedestrian. I ended up parking near the strip mall Joey was working at.

"Should we stop and say 'hi'?" Stella asked.

"Let's head downtown; we'll stop in on our way back." I said back.

To be honest, it was one of the most amazing festivals I had ever been to. The food was incredible, the wine vendors sold locally made wine and some of the arts and crafts they were selling were some of the most interesting finds.

When we reached the statue we froze and looked up in awe. It wasn't wonder but fear that throbbed in our chest when we looked at the giant black slab that jutted like a rotted tooth from the center of Park of America.

"What the hell is that?" I gasped.

Even though spotlights shined on it, it absorbed their light.

"Can you feel that?" Stella asked.

I could. The closer we got to the giant slab the more it thrummed inside me. A vibration that could only be felt inside.

"What do you think it is?" She asked me not taking her eyes off it.

"I···I'm not sure." We had walked closer to it and

the vibration was so bad it was hurting our teeth, "I don't think we should get any closer to it."

Our voices were being drowned out by the loud internal humming.

In front of it was a bronze plaque that read:

Lasciate ogne speranza, voi ch'intrate

"What does that mean?" Stella asked.

"You don't know it? It was written above the gate to Hell in Dante's Inferno." I said cleaning my glasses, "It's 'abandon all hope, ye who enter here' I believe."

"Jesus." She muttered.

With that the thrumming got stronger and blood spurt from her nose. She only stood staring at it.

The crowd had turned and looked towards us. I grabbed Stella's hand and began to walk her hurriedly towards our car.

The people only followed us with their eyes. It was almost as physical as that horrid vibration that coursed through us.

"How's your nose?" I asked.

She took her fingers away from it and it had stopped bleeding. But her face was caked with coagulated blood on her nose, lips and chin.

"Let's get you cleaned up, honey."

We were at our vehicle, but I led her to the salon Joe was working at. The door was locked but I banged on the door a few times before Joe came and let us in in a panic.

"What the fuck are you guys doing here?" he looked around before he locked the door back up, "I told you to stay home!"

He pulled the blinds on the salon. The air smelled of fresh paint with a hint of salon products in the background.

"What happened to you, Stella?" He asked sincerely worried, "Did they hit you?"

"No one hit her, Joe." I said, "But what the hell

is that thing out there in the middle of Park of America?"

He sat Stella down on one of the salon chairs and went to get a damp rag.

When he came back he looked even more upset.

"Did you guys touch it?" He asked.

"No, why?" I said.

"Good. Good. Although I don't think it is going to matter much soon."

"Joe, what the hell is that thing?"

He walked over to his tool bucket and pulled out a flask of Clan MacGreggor's Scotch and then dispensed three Dixie cups from the sink. He poured with a shaky hand.

"Do you remember Scott Finlay from school?" He asked, "Tall goofy fucker, came in half way through second semester?"

"Yeah, yeah." I did remember him, he was part of our circle of friends while we went to school, "He was in the marines. "

"Remember what happened to him?"

I thought back, it had been over 20 years.

"He disappeared. " Joe spoke up, "He met up with some chick, knocked her up, badda bing he was gone. "

"That's right. Shit, I had forgotten…"

"I bumped into him about a year ago. I was walking out of Billy Frogg's bar, took the alleyway to my car. He was just sitting there in the muck. He looked like shit. Scrawny. He looked like a damn meth head. "

"Was he on meth?"

"No. But he was on something. I tried to talk to him but he was out of it. Kept whispering to himself. Scared the shit out of me, actually.

"Then I got up and was going to call an ambulance or somethin'. But he grabbed my arm and pulled my face way down to his. Man, he stunk so bad. Like he had pissed and shit himself mixed with b.o. "

"What does this have to do with---?" I tried to ask

but he interrupted me.

"Just shut up and listen, okay?

"He said 'the coven owns the market'."

"' The coven'? What the hell is that supposed to mean?"

He looked at me curtly and then looked over at Stella and her cleaned face.

"He doesn't listen for shit, does he?" he asked her.

She only nodded in agreement. Bless her.

"I did some digging." He continued, "There is a coven of witches that own most of the businesses in the warehouse district. Essentially, they own most of the Old Market.

"These aren't the witches you see on T.V., these are wiccans. Or so I thought. According to a friend I know who does security for the buildings around here; this coven has been up to some clandestine shit.

"There have been ritual killings throughout the Omaha

area that no one has been able to solve. Domestic animals, children, and last week···they found Scotts body.

"They had mutilated his body and hung it on the Park of America Bridge."

"Jesus!" Stella said for a second time.

Joe's head swung around at her, "Be careful what you say, Stell, and be careful *where* you say it."

"Joey, this is crazy." I said to him pouring another nip.

"Really?" he said refilling his own, "That damn black thing shot up out of the ground overnight. Right after Scotts death. Bam! Just like that. No one knows where or how it got there; I even called some of the family in the O.P.D. and they told me to just leave it alone."

"Well, they have a plaque in front of it." I said.

"It's the gateway to hell, Jay." He was dead serious, and he was never dead serious.

"Why do you think its all 'Stepford' around here?" he continued. "That thing influences people. You both felt the···vibrations I'm sure?"

Stella crossed her arms as if she felt a chill and I nodded.

"Why did you invite us out here, Joey?" I asked.

"You're a reporter." He said, "I was hoping you could help expose what's going on in Omaha. But I think it's too late for that."

"What is going on in Omaha, Joey?"

"The end. They're getting ready for a big parade. Not just any parade, it's a parade to celebrate the coming of Lucifer. Bright angel of the sun. They used to only have influence downtown, but its spread into the suburbs."

"I thought your security had been acting a bit peculiar." I said.

"Shit!" he said, "Did they say anything to you?"

"Just asked us weird questions." Stella spoke up,

"I didn' t think he was going to let us out of your neighborhood. But he called someone and then let us out shortly after. We thought he was calling you. "

"It wasn' t me. " He said, "Shit! We need to get you guys out of here. "

"Settle down, Joey. " I said grabbing his arms, "Chill out. Maybe we can help. "

"No. They know you' re here, Jay. That' s not good. They' ll be coming for you. "

"Don' t be ridiculous. Some cult is going to come and kill Stella and I?"

"The only reason I' m alive right now, Jay, is because of my family name. But I think in the end, a Gnucci or an Obama, it' s not going to matter. "

"How long have you been hitting the sauce?"

"Goddammit, Jay, I' m not fucking around! With every sacrifice that thing is getting more and more powerful! The parade is tomorrow night! We' re out of time! We need to get out of town!"

Joey Gnucci had been my best friend for over 20 years. He had never steered me wrong; okay, maybe he gave certain girls he met MY number instead of his own and maybe he talked me into a few antics that landed us in jail overnight. But for the most part, he was always my wingman, and as crazy as he sounded that night. I believed him.

We came up with the plan that we would act natural and head to a motel. Just a road weary couple looking to sleep. Joey would then come and pick us up in the early morning about 4:30 a. m. and we would get out of the city limits together. He said he would alert his family that had connections on getting them out of the city. We hugged and parted company, acting like we just stopped in to say 'hello' and he acted like he was going back to work.

The desk clerk at the Red Roof Inn was surprised to see us. She kept asking how we made it past the detours and I told her I knew back roads from my college days. This seemed to satisfy her curiosity but she still didn't look happy to see us. I noticed there were other motorists who had checked in, since the parking lot was full.

We didn't unpack our bags. We set them close to the window for easy access.

"What the hell do we do until 4:30?" Stella asked pacing.

"Watch the t.v.?" I said getting up to stop her pacing, "It'll be okay, honey. That's only a few hours away. Let's just relax."

"How the hell do we relax? If what Joey said was true···my god! If what he says is true what are we going to do, Jay?"

"We'll figure that out when we get to it. I never believed in the end of the world mythos created by religion and superstition. That crap was just spoken to put fear into the populace to worship whatever god was head honcho at the time."

"Then explain to me, Professor Jay Christiansen; what is that thing out there in the park? Why does the damn thing vibrate like that? You know goddamn well there is something supernatural going on, don't deny it!"

"Keep your voice down. I can't explain half that shit. Only that cults run on fear, with today's technology; who knows what they're capable of creating. You can't let them know how much you're scared.

"Now come on. Lay down on the bed with me. We'll watch a little tele until Joe shows up, okay? Take a nap."

"I can't." she said as she lay against my side with her face resting on my chest.

It turned out she could. We both could.

We were awoken to the sound of someone rapping on the window. Stella jumped at the same time I did.

The clock read 4:40 a.m. I went over to the window and became alarmed when it wasn't Joey standing there in the shrubs outside. I slid the window open part ways.

"What do you want?" I whispered to the stranger.

"Jay and Stella Christiansen?" she whispered back.

"Maybe. Who the fuck are you?"

"Bethanie Gnucci. I'm Joey's cousin."

"Where's Joey?"

"Waiting for us. Come on."

"He never said anything about--- "

"We don't have much time, Jay. They're already collecting people from the hotels."

Stella reluctantly went through the window with me. We put our luggage in the back of Bethanie's Lexus.

A loud horn echoed through the sky like a giant throb. I thought my head was going to explode. Stella and I had both collapsed to the ground.

"What the fuck was that?" I said.

"They're here." Bethanie shouted.

From around the corner a metro bus hissed to a stop.

"What's going on?" Stella asked.

Bethanie tasered me. I heard Stella try to attack her and then a loud thump and my wife was lying unconscious beside me on the concrete.

"Stella?" I said.

Then something from above me came down on my head. I didn't have time to register what it was. A sharp pain, my ears rang, there were stars and then blackness.

When I came to, there was movement. As if we were riding in a hay wagon on a bumpy gravel road. I could feel a breeze blow the top of my hair, and when I opened my eyes I realized I was riding in what seemed to be a hay wagon. My legs and arms were zip-stripped and tethered to the wagon floor.

There were several of us on the cart which was hitched to other carts. I couldn't see Stella. She wasn't on my cart and she didn't seem to be on any nearby.

On each cart was a police officer with a shotgun at the ready. My fellow passengers were just as frightened as I was.

We were parked alongside one another inside a giant

warehouse. I think, if memory serves me well, we were inside one of the old stockyard barns. We could all smell the rotted meat coming from the ground.

"Ladies and gentlemen." A male voice spoke from above, "We would like to welcome you to the beginning of the end. Tonight is a special night, one that will go down in history. You are about to witness the coming of Lucifer. The one true God of earth as foretold in the ancient texts.

"You will be brought through the streets of our festival to witness the rituals needed to bring our king to rule. At the end of your journey you will be sacrificed to bring about the key to unlock the abyss. Praise him!!"

The other people who weren't bound to the trailers went into some orgasmic chants of worship to Lucifer.

The giant doors to the pens opened and the tractors pulling us roared to life. We all jerked and then looked in horrified anxiety to see what awaited us beyond those great doors.

It was like a parade of sorts. Crowds were gathered at

either end of the streets cheering. Streamers and balloons floated in the night air. Children danced and skipped along the hay wagons singing.

But there was no candy being thrown from these morbid floats, only cries for help. There were no high school bands marching through a popular song put to band music. The words on the banners were blasphemies to God and hails to Satan. The revelers were hardly clothed, enacting obscenities to one another in the public eye. All the while the vibration thrummed stronger and louder in everyone's heads.

Some of us on the wagons began to cry and scream as we passed by murders being performed on the sidewalks as we passed. Still, no sign of Joey or Stella.

The streets were running red with the blood of those unlucky enough be caught by the crowds. Depending on how you look at it, I guess they were the lucky ones in hindsight. But hindsight is always 20/20, as they say.

We came to a stop in front of that great monolith. Gathered there were twelve robed women. A coven; and tied to posts were Stella and Joe. Joe was hanging upside down on a cross. The women disrobed and gathered around Joe who was screaming from the pain of having his wrists hammered into the upside down crucifix.

Each woman produced a large serrated blade and sliced his guts open. They moaned loudly in ecstasy and the crowd followed in suit and they rubbed his innards all over their nakedness.

I screamed out to Stella but the crowd was so loud that she couldn't hear me. One of the witches walked over to her and kissed her on her lips to muffle her screams and then plunged the blade into her chest, churning the blade until she could reach into my wife's chest and pull out her heart.

The witch raised it to the monolith and then squeezed it until all that blood drenched her face around her mouth.

I screamed uncontrollably, muffled by the crowd and then suddenly, the vibration that emitted from the monolith was threatening to split my skull in half.

That obsidian rock rumbled and began to shift. As if it were a black sheet being pulled in the middle. It was imploding within itself. I could feel myself being drawn towards it like a heavy pull of gravity. All of us were being pulled towards it. The hay wagons we were on were skidding on the cobblestone street.

Then, it seemed like all the air was sucked out of the area. Silence was deafening. Something blazed from the sky and was absorbed into the rock. As the air rushed back, I felt the pressure in my ears and head, my nose began bleeding and the wagons fell back shattering the bonds that were holding us.

I stumbled to my feet only to witness the rock and the space around it disappearing within itself. The gaping hole where the rock stood spat out molten earth and the smell of sulfur gushed into our nostrils.

From the depths I could hear something coming. Something that growled an inhuman voice. Behind that growl was the chorus of snarls getting louder as they reached the surface of the lava flow.

I turned and ran.

I made it as far as Greives, NE on foot. How I made it as far as I did is beyond me. Perhaps it was my grief that gave me the adrenaline to push forth. Why I headed west also escapes me.

Once the gate opened, everything changed. The sky turned a dark red like the color of blood. Motorized vehicles died on the spot as soon as the wave of darkness washed over them. There were traffic jams and thousands of motorists exiting from their vehicles.

There was a silence, as all of us looked at what our world had become. It was only a matter of an hour when they came. Demons. Black wisps of negative energy ripping through the Nebraska countryside seeking vessels to inhabit and torture. So many fell. The ones that weren't possessed, were eaten by those that were.

I hid. Here in this old warehouse that is covered with vines and graffiti. I haven't had the time or energy to grieve the loss of my wife, or my friend, or even life as I knew it. I had to be silent, and was lucky to find this old Nebraskan township that perhaps was once a booming town but now only held a few rural citizens within its borders.

It's only now at this moment....that I realize....this typing beating out a rat-a-tat-tat upon these old sheets of paper...has only given me away. The shadows grow darker. The air is colder. Something is behi

MR. MATTHEWS CHECKS OUT

As with the majority of my stories, this one stemmed from a dream I had. Not sure what it meant, only that I had to write it down. So if the entire read seems obscure like a Dali painting…well, blame my medications.

"Can I help you, brother?" the desk clerk, dressed in black; looked like the lizard king himself.

"Yeah," Mr. Matthews answered nervously, "I wanna check out."

"Whatcher name?" he opened the registry.

"Uh...Matthews...Henry Matthews."

"Matthews, eh?" a smile lit on his lips as he looked through the dusty ledger.

After a while, Henry Matthews started tapping his fingers on the desk in front of him.
The desk clerk looked up at him through that graying brown mane of hair.

"Sorry." Henry said not really meaning it. He was irritated and didn't have the patience allotted to gentlemen of his stature.

82

The clerk smiled with a Cheshire grin when he got to the last page and then snapped the heavy cover shut.

"*What?*" Henry asked annoyed by that perma-smile on the clerks full lips.

"Can't help you, Mr. Matthews." he said with a nod.

"What do you mean 'you can't help me'?" Matthews spat, "I want to check out!"

"Listen, listen, man. Ain't no checkin out unless your names on the register...so...uh...head over to the hotel bar...grab some tacos and a mai tai....and boogie on up to yer room...take it easy...and think about what yer doin..."

"That's fucked up!"

"Everything is fucked up, brother; just do what I said...you'll feel better about it."

"I'm checking out."
"Nope. 'fraid not."

Henry turned and went to go out the front door. As he went through the doorway he ended up back in his hotel room.

"Jesus fuck!" Mr. Matthews shouts to himself.

He picked up the phone and dialed "0".

"Front desk, Mr. Matthews, how can I help you?"

"The *hell* kind of place is this?"

"I told you to head to the bar first, man...you just don't listen."

"But I walked out the front door...and...and..."

"Doors are funny things, ain't they?"

"Goddammit, all I want to do is check out of this roach hotel!!"

Laughter followed his rant. It wasn't contagious laughter, it was the kind that felt mocking and pissed a person off.

"What's so fucking funny? I just want to check out!! Is that so hard??"

There was a click on the other end.

He went to the sliding glass door of his room and pulled back the drapes. The night sky was littered with stars. Planets orbited an invisible sun. It was a giant vacuum of airless oblivion. He snapped the latch on the handle, and slid open the door. A loud sucking noise ripped through the air, pulling his skin from his bones out into the void. It was sweet and he savored the moment as he felt his life fleeting from himself.

Then there was a loud "pop" and he felt as if he had been slapped by a giant cosmic hand and opened his eyes. Henry Matthews was standing in front of the goddamn desk clerk again.

"Name?" asked the desk clerk dressed in black.

"Matthews...um..weren't we just going over this?"

That damn smile came back on his mouth, "Procedure, Hank, everything has rules and regulations...you know that."

Henry didn't like being called 'Hank'. His own father used to call him that and he thought it cheapened his moniker; "Look, just let me check out!"

"Family?"

"I'm sorry...what?"

"Family, Hank...do you have a wife?"

"Ummm...yes?" he answered, but he somehow knew that living image of Jim Morrison knew the answer already.

He scribbled in the registry. Henry hated it when people scribbled in notebooks when they were talking to you. Like therapists, doctors, lawyers.

"Do you have kids with this wife?"

He felt a sharp stab in his heart, "Two. Michael and....and...Allison."

The clerk put down his pen, ran his hands through his long shaggy hair and sighed.
"Can't let you check out, Mr. Matthews."

"But but but...I..."

"Nope. You need to go on up to your room. There is no
checking out. This is where you are needed."

He lowered his head in defeat.

"Very well." and he made his way to the stairs.

"Chin up, Mr. Matthews. When you are feelin better...come
back down to the bar...I'm singing there nightly. Maybe we
can have a mai tai together?"

Henry Matthews went up to his room. 332. He slipped his
key card through the slot. Twice, because they never work
the first time through; He turned the handle and took a deep
breath and opened the door.

"Daddy?" came his kids' voice, "can we go swimming now?"

A smile returned to his lips. It almost felt ancient but it was
familiar.

"Yes, of course we can...grab some towels."

They cheered as his wife came out of the rest room dressed
in that great bikini he's always loved her in.

"What took you?" she asked.

"I'm sorry, honey. I got lost." He kissed her like he did on
the day they were married, "Where's my trunks?"

KELSO'S PUMP AND GO

Any of you smokers out there ever try Chantix to quit smoking? Well, the product does work but there's a nasty side effect: vivid dreams. I had some of the bloodiest dreams on that junk. I asked the doctor about it and he said you will either have vivid erotic dreams or vivid nightmare's. Of course, you know what I got stuck with. I can't imagine what I'd come up with if it were the other way around....

The Saturn chugged for about 38 miles south of Sioux City on I-29. Mark had filled the tank but it was acting as if the fuel pump was clogged.

He dialed his mother's number in Omaha but she didn't answer. He grit his teeth as he felt the engine lose power and it began to stall.

"Son of a bitch!" He screamed to himself as he coasted into the shoulder. He pulled a Marlboro out of his breast pocket and lit it.

He dialed his mother again. As she picked up he heard a rumble like thunder behind him. A familiar sound of Harley Davidsons coming south. It was normal, as the annual biker fest in Sturgis had just ended another week of debauchery.

"Hello?" his mother repeated.

"Ma!" he shouted over the rumble. He noticed close to 30 bikes pulling over in the shoulder with him.

"Yes, son, what is it?"

He looked into his rearview mirror and saw there must have been another 40 bikes behind him in the shoulder.

"Shit." He said to himself.

"What?"

"Oh, sorry, Ma. Look, I'm having car trouble. So I...."

He read the back of the leather vests. HELL'S ANGELS MASSACHUSETTES

"Son, are you okay?"

"Um, sorry, Ma. I'm going to have to go."

"Mark?"

He hangs up on his mother and looks around for a weapon.

"Son of a bitch." He says again to himself, "I'm going to die."

He jumps and nearly wets himself as a surprise knock raps on his window. It's one of the bikers. Long dusty hair and an even longer beard. A blue bandana faded with years of sweat and sunshine wrapped around a sunburnt brow. But he is smiling.

Mark cracks the window.

"Hey, man, everything okay?" the biker asks.

"Um." Mark says, "The damn thing keeps stalling. It starts back up after I let it sit awhile."

"Sounds like your fuel line. Hang tight, I'll be right back."

The biker walks towards the back of the line and Mark sees him chatting with another biker. The other biker nods his head and then kick starts his bike and it roars to life. He pulls out from the shoulder and roars on to the next exit.

The original biker walks back to his window.

"Shot Glass will be right back." He says, "We'll get you going again."

"You guys don't really need to...." Mark begins.

"Naw, man, it's cool. Hate seein' anyone stalled on a desolate interstate like this. Especially in a cage."

"Cage?"

"Yeah, man, cage. That's what you're drivin'."

"Oh, the car?"

"You got it."

Mark lit another cigarette. "Want one?"

"Naw, thanks, I quit about 3 years ago."

"Good for you."

"So, uh, where you headed?"

"Omaha. Visiting my parents."

The biker just nodded his head and then walked up to his own hog and laid one on his "old lady".

Mark's mother called him again.

"Hey, Ma." He said.

"What's going on?" she asked worried, "Are you okay?"

"Yeah, car stalled. Some nice...uh...bikers stopped and are helping me get it fixed."

"Bikers?"

"It's okay, Ma, really. I won't make it home for lunch but I should be there before dinner."

"Just be careful, Mark."

They said their good-byes and hung up. Mark raised his Galaxy 3 and snapped a photo of the crowd of bikers parked in front of him. He fiddled around with menus and then posted the photo on his

Facebook page.

"This is how Iowa does emergency road service" he wrote, and added, *"Feeling-nervous :/"*

At that moment there was another rap on his window. It was a different biker, and he didn't look very happy.

"Yeah?" Mark said timidly.

"Erase that photo." The biker ordered him.

"What?"

"That photo you just took, erase it...NOW!"

"I'm sorry." He fumbled through his phone's gallery.

"Gimme that goddamn thing!"

The biker snatched it out of his sweaty hands and touched a few buttons on his touchscreen and deleted his photo. He then began to peruse the photos taken in his gallery.

"Can I have that back?" Mark asked nervously.

"Hang on." The biker stopped at one photo and smiled, "Who's the hot chick?"

"Uh…um…that is my sister."

"NICE! I bet I could have a lot of fun with that!"

"Now that's not necessary. Just hand me my phone back."

The biker laughed and then handed the phone back to him. When Mark reached for it, the biker snatched it back.

"Please, sir."

"Did you post that picture on anything?"

"What?"

"What? Don't be a dumbfuck, you heard what I said."

Mark thought about lying to him. But then realized the guy would only have to touch the Facebook icon on his phone and he'd be on his page.

He already felt violated enough.

"I....I'm sorry, I posted it to my Facebook page."

The biker handed him the phone, "Take it off. I'm gonna stand right here and watch you do it."

With hands trembling, Mark deleted his Facebook post. The biker leaned into his window still glaring at him.

"Listen. Some of us don't like being photographed. Especially by cumlickers like you. So keep your phone to yourself until we get you up and runnin', or I'll come back here and shove that phone so far up your ass you'll be able to dial out with your tongue. Comprende?"

Mark nodded his head and waited until the biker walked away before he breathed again. He wanted to start his car and leave, but he knew the bikers would just chase him down and if the Saturn has been reliable for anything, it's breaking down.

The biker who had left pulled up and parked his bike right in front of him. He banged on his hood.

"What?" Mark asked.

The biker held up a can of Seafoam engine cleaner.

"C'mon, open that hood!" The biker yelled.

Mark popped the hood and stepped out of his vehicle.

"Can I help?" Mark asked.

"Just hang tight in your cage, little man." The biker said as he uncapped the engine block, "I've got some medicine for your engine and a can of medicine for your fuel injector."

The first biker walked up to him.

"Don't worry, man." He said patting him on the shoulder, "Shot Glass is our mechanic."

After Shot Glass finished capping the engine

block, he slammed the hood and then told Mark to start his car and made his way to the fuel tank with another can of Seafoam injector cleaner.

The Saturn started right up. Relief flooded into Mark's face and the bikers started their bikes and drove off giving him the thumbs up.

He lit another Marlboro and exhaled deeply releasing a giant plume of smoke. He checked his side view mirror and pulled back out onto I-29 and clicked on his radio.

#

60 miles before hitting the Council Bluffs/Omaha border, the Saturn began to chug again. Sputtering and dying and then revving up again.

He stomped his foot to the floor with the accelerator, it sputtered and then yanked it's way forward.

"C'mon, girl!" Mark shouted at his dash, "C'mon, we're almost there!"

But "she" didn't listen and decided to die at mile marker 83. There was an off ramp that led off into the bluffs to a small town called Abaddon, Iowa.

Mark dialed his parent's house and his dad answered.

"Dad," Mark said slightly happy. "I really need your help. The car broke down again near someplace called Abaddon in Iowa right off I-29. Do you think you could come and get me?"

"Abaddon?" His dad asked, "Never heard of it. Can't you just call a tow truck?"

"I guess, but, can't you guys come and get me and I can have someone nearby fix it and we can get it on my way back home?"

"I've already had a few beers, I probably shouldn't."

"What's Ma doin?"

"She's makin' dinner. Are you going to make it in time for dinner?"

"Obviously, not, dad. Since no one can come and get me."

Mark could hear his mother's voice in the background and then his dad spoke up, "Hang on, your mom wants to talk to you."

"Mark?" she said.

"Mom! Do you think you could come out to Abaddon in Iowa to get me? My car broke down again."

"I told you I didn't trust those bikers."

"Right, so...can you come and get me?"

"I can't leave dinner on the stove while it's cooking."

Mark let out a deep sigh, "Okay, can you come and get me after dinner?"

"Oh, so you're not coming to dinner?"

"Jesus! I'm stalled on the side of the fucking road in bumfuck, Iowa! How the hell am I going to make it home for dinner?"

"Mark Connor O'Hare! You watch your mouth when talking to your mother!!"

"Sorry, Ma."

"Don't you sorry me! You've never spoke to me like that before! It's that damn lifestyle your living! I told you that God would bring bad things on you if you turned gay!"

Mark felt another battery of curse words load into his mouth and he swallowed them down and lit another cigarette.

"Ma," he said as calmly as he could. "Can you come and get me or not?"

His phone beeped twice signifying his battery life was at 10%.

"Ma," he pleaded. "I need to know soon. My battery is dying on my phone and my charger doesn't work when the car isn't running."

"Call us when you get your car into the shop." She says, "I'll send dad up to get you."

"He's been drinking, Ma."

His phone warns him again, this time it's at 6%. The battery drains faster when he's roaming.

"Okay, I'll call you when I get towed. Bye."

He lets out a deep sigh and then uses another 2% of his battery life to find a tow service. Then 3% to call the tow service and he sits with the remaining 1% as he attempts to start his car so that he can run his charger.

As luck would have it, Kelso's Pump and Go was in the town of Abaddon which was only 6 miles from Interstate 29. They had their own tow truck and sent it out lickety split.

The tow truck driver introduced himself as Cameron Kelso, but everyone just called him "Cam". He dressed in oil stained blue coveralls that were ripped in various places. His hair looked just as oily with an outcrop of patchy reddish-brown facial hair. He made a few adjustments with the hitch and within 5 minutes, Mark's Saturn was up in the air and ready to go to the car doctor.

The truck was old, 1960's model Mark figured. It smelled of grease and stale cigarettes.

"Do you mind if I smoke?" Mark asked, "It's been a really long day."

"Go for it." Cam answered pulling out a cancer stick of his own and lighting it.

"So what do you think it is?"

"Hard to tell until I can look at it. Sounds like it could be your fuel pump."

"There were some bikers who put Seafoam in

the engine for me, it worked pretty good for a while, but then it started up again."

"Where you headed?"

"Omaha. I'm visiting my parents."

"That's not too far then."

"I was hoping I could use your phone to call them when we get to your shop."

"Well, we don't carry long distance on our phone. So, you would have to call them collect. Don't you have a cell phone?"

"Yeah, but the battery is almost dead. Maybe I could plug my charger in to your cigarette lighter?"

"Doesn't work, man, sorry."

"That's okay."

Mark thought about it, and he thought he just saw Cam light his cigarette with the cigarette lighter.

There wasn't much to Abaddon, Iowa. There was a lot of abandoned buildings of what Mark guessed was once a sprawling community. The only thing with any life in it was the bar that looked more like someone's trailer with a Coors Lite sign in it.

Around the corner was Kelso's Pump and Go. An old stucco building with a double garage and two old style pumps. There was a second story with boarded up windows.

"Here we are!" Cam announced.

He slowly backed his Saturn into the garage. There were two others inside the garage. Another guy dressed in oily blues and a woman with tufts of red hair tucked into a green bandana.

Mark hopped out of the tow truck and walked into the small waiting room/lobby of the station. There were a few old snack foods on dusty shelves and an old Pepsi machine selling soda for .50 cents. He walked up to the counter and there was an old man sitting at a desk watching a small black and white television.

"Um, excuse me?" Mark said.

The old man looked up, "Oh, sorry! Get a little involved when Wheel of Fortune is on. How can I help ya?"

"Yeah, I was wondering if I can use your phone. I need to call my parents in Omaha."

"Omaha? I don't carry long distance on my phone because most people have cell phones now and frankly, it's cheaper."

"My cellphone is dead and I don't have a way to charge it."

"I can charge your phone for you?" said a female voice from behind him.

"Excuse me?" Mark turned around.

"I've got a charger upstairs." It was the female mechanic, "I can plug it for you."

"That's very kind, but I don't want to be any

trouble...."

"No trouble, sugar." She said flirtatiously, and grabbed his phone from him.

"Thank you."

"My name's Heidi Kelso."

"Heidi."

They pump hands and she takes his phone upstairs.

"Ack, that girl." The old man says under his breath, "She gets a little too friendly sometimes."

"Don't worry, sir." Mark said uneasily, "Your daughter is safe around me. I bat for the other team, if you catch what I mean."

The old man looks at Mark for a moment as if he is dissecting him with his eyes.

"I figured." The old man says, "Saw that rainbow sticker on your bumper. Makes no difference to me, long as you don't go puttin' your hands on me."

"Um, okay, promise." Mark smiled.

The old man offered his hand, "My name's Gale Kelso. I own this place. You met my sons Cameron and Gale Jr."

"Yeah. So I was hoping to call my folks so they could give me a ride back until you get my car fixed."

"I see your predicament."

"They were expecting me for dinner."

"You could have dinner with us!" Heidi said behind him again, "We're about an hour from eating."

"I....uh, I don't want to impose on...."

"Nonsense!" Gale said, "I insist."

"You don't suppose I could call my parents collect from your phone?" Mark asked.

Heidi walked in front of him and pulled her bandana from her head. Red ringlets of long hair fell down on her shoulders.

"Oh, just stay for dinner." She said, "We can have your car running by the time you finish dessert."

Mark let out a sigh and shook his head in agreement, "If you think you can have my car fixed?"

"Cam! Junior!" Gale shouted into the garage, "Think we can have our gay friend's car going after dinner?"

They both looked at each other and then at Mark.

"Sure!" Cam said, "When's dinner?"

#

A half hour later, Mark was lead upstairs to the upper apartment. At the top of the stairs was a small hallway where everyone took off their blue overalls and the door opened into a big apartment.

There was plastic on the floors and blue tarps hung on ropes to divide the large space into smaller makeshift rooms.

"We're remodeling." Heidi said with a smile, "Follow me to the kitchen while everyone washes up."

The "kitchen" was a small windowless room. A large washtub served as a sink and a long metal table with a white sheet covering it. A crock pot sat atop the table with something steaming and smelling wonderful.

"Have a seat." Gale said sitting in his spot at the head of the table.

Mark looked at all the chairs, "Um, is there reserved seats?"

"Sit anywhere you're comfortable."

He sat down near Gale and the other two boys sat in the other seats leaving the other end of the table open for Heidi.

"What would you like to drink, sugar?" Heidi

asked.

"Uh, what do you have?" Mark asked.

She opened the old refrigerator, "Looks like I've got two Mountain Dews left, a pitcher of iced tea, and milk."

"I'll take some iced tea, please."

"So," Mark looked over at Cam. "Is it the fuel pump?"

Cameron looked confused and then said, "Oh, yeah. Looks like it's a bit gunked up. Don't know when your last oil change was, but judging by how dirty it is under the hood, it's been awhile."

Mark blushed in embarrassment.

"You know, that's the cheapest thing you can do to keep your car runnin." Junior spoke up, sounding a little aggressive.

"I....I know. I feel like an idiot."

"You are." Junior said back.

"Don't mind him." Heidi said placing a tall glass of iced tea in front of him, "He loves cars so much he will never have a girlfriend."

Mark guzzled the iced tea, "May have some more? I'm really thirsty, sorry."

"Oh, don't worry. Of course you can."

Heidi poured him another tall glass.

Mark gulped down another glass. He was thirsty, he had smoked several cigs and cotton mouth was his new best friend.

He looked around at the table and noticed that everyone was staring in his direction.

"What's everyone looking at?" He asked, "Haven't you ever seen a gay man before?"

He suddenly felt drunk and a little silly. He thought for sure they were all laughing.

"Hope you didn't give him too much." Cam said in a voice that sounded to Mark like it was in a long echoing cave.

"You might kill him." Junior said in the same hollow voice.

The room began to spin and Mark tried to stand up. He tried to lean against the spinning room and the plastic covered floor found his face with a crunch.

"I....think....I'm going to..." Mark said and then vomited.

Shortly after, his lights went out.

"Glad we put the plastic down." Gale said, "C'mon, boys, get him up. I'll clear the table."

#

Mark awoke to the sensation of something pulling at his arm. He opened his eyes and at first, everything was blurry.

He tried to get up but his hands would lift up from where they were, and his torso was held by some sort of strap.

His vision began to clear and he saw the Kelso family gathered around him. He was strapped to the metal table that served as the dining room table. Gale was holding a long knife that had blood dripping from it.

"What...." His mouth felt full of cotton still, "What the fuck is....going on?"

"You are one tasty motherfucker!" Laughed Junior.

"Actually," Cameron added. "He's gay....so he would be a 'fatherfucker'!"

The whole family laughed loudly. Mark looked down at his right arm and they had carved a long chunk out of his arm.

"Are you.....are.....are you fuckers eating me???" He whimpered.

"Don't worry, sissyboy," Cameron said. "We

gave you a big dose of Novocain, you won't feel a thing!"

They all laughed and then they took a slice off the other arm. He felt that same awful pulling and he thought he would go mad watching them. They laid both slices of him on a silver platter.

His arms were soaked with blood and he was able to pull his arms free of their bonds. He sat up quickly and realized whatever roofie they slipped him was going to make balance difficult.

"Ooooo, he's getting' free!!" Junior squealed.

He heard sizzling coming from the other side of a sheet and as he rounded the corner the smell of his own cooking flesh permeated his nostrils and he almost stopped to puke. Junior grabbed onto his arm directly on the wound and Mark cried out in pain. There was too much blood and his grip slipped and Mark yanked his arm free and ran down the hallway.

"Don't let that gay sumbitch get away!" Gale cried out.

Mark made his way to the staircase and was met by Cameron.

"The fuck you think you're going?" Cameron snarled blocking his way.

Mark screamed out and tackled him down the stairs. He felt every agonizing step as his raw nerve endings hit each stair.

They both splayed out at the bottom of the stairs in a pile of metal that was a shelf that held motor oil.

"Stay the fuck away from me!" Mark shouted trying to get to his feet.

"Can't let my dinner get away from me!" Cameron grinned at him as he staggered towards him.

As Cameron lunged at him he picked up a

jagged piece of metal from the shelf and held it out.

Cameron ran straight into it, impaling his chest

deeply. The look of surprise on his face made Mark

gag as blood bubbled out of his mouth and he

dropped to the ground.

"Motherfucker!" Heidi screeched as she

jumped at him from the 4th stair.

Mark put his arms up in defense and she bit

down into the raw meat of his forearm. He screamed

out and delivered a painful roundhouse to her

temple. Still, her teeth stayed embedded into his arm.

"Let me go!!" He shouted as he repeatedly

punched her temple.

She growled at him in defiance.

He grabbed the side of her hair and then

plunged his thumb into her eye socket, grimacing as

he heard her eye squishing and then made a wet

popping sound. She bit down harder on his muscle

tissue but he was able to rip it free from her grip.

He started to get up but she had wrapped her legs around his waist and began squeezing as she cupped her ruined eye.

He found a bottle of oil and struck her several times in the face with it until she loosened her grip on him. Panic struck him as he heard Gale and Junior coming down the steps, so he got to his feet and ran into the garage where his car was still up on the lift.

"Fuck me!" he muttered and then made a break for the door.

He ran to the tow truck and prayed the keys were in it. He slammed the door closed and locked both and searched frantically for the keys. Junior and Gale were coming out the garage with a large crescent wrench and a rubber mallet.

"You ain't goin' nowhere, you fucking faggot!" Gale yelled as they approached.

He looked in the glove box when Junior came down with the rubber mallet on the passenger side window. It spider-webbed and then another blow from Gale with the wrench on the driver's side. It splintered and Mark checked the visor and a pair of keys dropped onto the floor of the cab.

"Little pig, little pig," Junior mocked. "Let me in!!"

With that, the passenger side window crashed in. Mark found the keys and slipped them into the ignition. The driver's side window crashed and his face was nicked with broken glass.

Gale reached in and tried to stop him from starting the truck but it roared victoriously to life. He punched the clutch tried to look for reverse when Junior reached in and tried to grab the gear shift from him.

Mark grabbed a pen he found on the floor and

stabbed him clumsily in the cheek. Junior cried out and backed out of the cab. He found reverse and punched the accelerator. Gravel flew up in a rooster tail making Gale and his namesake run for cover.

The Novocain was beginning to wear off and it was painful to operate the truck. Wincing and gritting his teeth he pulled out onto the street and made his way out of town and to the Interstate.

By the time he made it to the Iowa/Nebraska border his arms were throbbing angrily. His adrenaline was wearing down and the pain was amplifying. He pulled the tow truck over just on the Nebraska side of the Mormon Bridge and wrapped his forearms in greasy rags he found in the cab of the truck. He took spare wiring he found on the floor and used it as a tourniquet just below his elbows.

He put the truck into gear and began to pull out onto Interstate 680 when the same group of bikers pulled up to him and surrounded his truck. Exhausted, he pulled back into the shoulder and put on the parking brake.

The lead biker poked his head into the window, "Holy shit, man! What happened to you?"

"Crazy son-of-a-bitches tried to eat me." He said as unconsciousness tried to claim him.

"Guess that explains the tow truck. Need to get you to the hospital, dude."

The biker looked at the makeshift bandages and all the blood, he motioned for his second in command to come take a look.

"Fuck!" the other biker said and opened Mark's door, "Move over, man, I'm driving you to the hospital!"

"I just want to get ho….." blackness overtook him.

Mark awoke in the ICU of Creighton Medical Center. The room lit by the tiny LED's of his monitors. His rags replaced by gauze and a good dose of morphine kept his pain at bay. Next to his bed was a biker. He was watching "The Price Is Right" and then looked over at him.

"Hey, man." He said sitting up, "You doin' okay?"

"Where am I?" Mark asked groggily.

"Creighton Medical. Got you all patched up, and doped up."

"Do my parents know I'm here?"

"Nope. You didn't have your phone on you. So really, had no idea how to get ahold of them."

"Can you hand me the phone?"

The biker handed him the hospital bed phone and he dialed his parent's number. It rang three times and then his mother picked it up.

"Mom!" Mark said almost coming to tears, "Mom!"

"Calm down, son." She said, "What's wrong? Where are you? Are you still in Abaddon?"

"No! God, no! I'm in the hospital. Can you come get me?"

"The hospital? Why are you in the hospital?"

"Just..." the memory of the previous night made him shiver, "Just come get me, please."

"Well, I've got some shopping to do. Maybe your dad can come and get you. Hang on..."

He can hear his mother explain to his dad that he is in the hospital. No, she didn't know why he was in there. No, he apparently didn't have his car. No, he hasn't given any details about what's going on. No, she can't get him because she promised to go shopping with Andrea from next door. His dad mumbles something unintelligible.

"It might be awhile," she comes back on. "Your father has a few errands to run first. Plus, you know he's got to have his morning coffee with his retired buddies."

"Just forget it." Mark said bitterly, "I'll figure something else out."

"Well, don't get so impatient, Mark. You know, your father and I have lives too."

Mark hung up the phone. The biker looked a little concerned and then returned the phone to the night stand.

"Everything all right?" The biker asked.

"Think you can give me a lift back to my parent's house?" Mark asked.

"Sure, man, but you'll have to ride bitch on my bike. We dumped the tow truck in the river; Figured it was hot and someone might be looking for it."

Mark shivered again thinking about the

Kelso's.

"They must have really fucked you up?" the biker asked.

"They tried to fucking eat me!" Mark said bitterly.

"Who? The people at the garage?"

"Yes!"

"C'mon, man, seriously? That sounds like something out of a horror flick."

"They...they drugged me. When I woke up they had strapped me to the table and were carving strips of meat off my arms to cook and eat them."

"What the fuck???"

Mark laid there trembling, staring at his bandaged arms. There was dried blood still stuck in his nails.

"Let me talk to Double A, and we'll get goin', okay?"

The biker left the room and Mark started to put his clothes on.

Fifteen minutes later, Double A came in with a few of his club members looking concerned.

"Hey, Mark." Double A said, "Tooter told me what happened to you. Fuck, man, you're tougher than I thought. You need us to pay those crazy fucks a visit?"

"No, man." Mark said finishing getting dressed, "I just want to go home."

"Tooter is my man-at-arms. I'm going to have him give you a lift home."

"Thanks, man."

"Hey," Double A says shaking his hand. "You've got some cojones for a gay guy. You've got my respect. Take care, man.

"Tooter, drop him off then meet us at O.P.'s."

The group left in a thunderous roar and

headed to their 'clubhouse' in Council Bluffs, Iowa.

Tooter and Mark made it into the suburb of Millard and down his parent's street. As they rounded the corner of Washington Circle Mark's heart froze.

"Your car's here." Tooter said to him slowing down a few houses away.

Mark sat in frozen silence.

"Let's go check it out."

"No! No, I can't! Let's just go!"

"Don't worry, buddy, I'm carrying."

They pulled up to his parent's driveway. His Saturn sat ominously at the end of the drive. The house looked quiet.

"Fuck it, man." Mark said, "Let's just go!"

"Chill, you wounded them didn't you?" Tooter said, "I got your back!"

Mark thought about running as Tooter dropped the kickstand.

They walked cautiously up the cement steps to his parent's cookie cutter split-level home. Tooter drew his .45 caliber and slowly opened the front door.

"Stay behind me, man." He said, "And stay close."

"How did they find out where my parent's lived?" Mark whispered.

"Shhh."

Tooter opened the front door slowly. All the shades were drawn in the house and all the lights were turned down. It was near pitch black inside.

"This is a fucking trap." Mark whispered harshly.

"Shut the fuck up, Mark!" Tooter scolded, and they began to ascend the stairs.

When they reached the top floor landing the

first thing they found was his mother's dog, a lasa apso, lying crushed at the top of the steps. Blood had dried in a stain on the carpet.

"Jesus!" Mark gasped, "Spunky!"

They checked the living room and kitchen and then moved slowly down the hall to the bedrooms. There was nothing out of the ordinary.

Tooter made it back to the top of the stairs and motioned down the steps.

They descended into the basement. The family room was lit by candles. There were plastic tarps spread out on the floor and walls, but otherwise empty.

They backtracked to the door into the tuck under garage. Tooter raised his gun and turned the doorknob.

There was a loud crunching sound followed immediately by Tooter letting out a gurgling

"Urrrrkkk!"

He dropped his pistol and then his body went limp still an upright position.

"Tooter?" Mark asked.

His body jerked forward into the door, then back again, then with a sudden slam; his protector fell into a heap in front of the door.

"Jesus, Tooter, are you okay?"

The only reply was familiar laughter on the other side of the door.

"Welcome home, son!" Gale's voice came through the other side.

Mark shivered and then went to the floor looking for the .45 his late friend had dropped. The door opened on the other side but was immediately stopped by Tooter's body. Panicked, Mark found the gun and fired two rounds at the door.

"You wanna play rough, eh, faggot?" Gale said

from the opening.

Just then, a long sharpened metal rod came through the door and almost impaled him had he been 3 inches to the left.

"You fuckers!!" Mark screamed at them and fired off 5 more rounds.

Silence answered him on the other side of the door. He didn't want to peak his head into the opening and get his head impaled by the pole. He waited them out.

"Come on in, sugar." It was Heidi's voice. So he must have hit the old man, which left Junior to be accounted for.

"Fuck you, you one-eyed bitch!" Mark spat back at her.

"Tsk. Tsk. Tsk. That is no way to talk to a lady. Your mama was polite all the way to the end. Nice lady, a little plump, but very nice. Even when we were slicing her up."

"You fucking bitch! I'm going to kill you!"

"Oh, baby, I'm going to *eat* you. When we finish with you then we'll have some of your parents."

Mark let off two more rounds and then listened. The shots ringing in his ears in this enclosed space. He stood up and began to walk up the steps. He was going to try and make it to the neighbors and call the police.

As he made it to the first step, the long iron rod shot out through the small gap in the door and punctured his left thigh and he fell forward onto his face.

"I got 'em, daddy!" Junior giggled like a mad man.

"Daddy's almost dead." Heidi replied, "Just pull that little fucker in here!"

Junior grabbed ahold of his ankle through the opening and dragged him painfully through it. Mark twisted so he could defend himself but Heidi was already on top of him, knees pressing into the meat of his already ruined arms.

He could see the bodies of his parents lying in a pile on the floor. They had been field dressed like a deer would be.

"Grab his arm." Heidi ordered Junior, "Take off those bandages."

Gale Kelso was lying next to him with a gunshot wound to his neck. He was bleeding out, staring emotionless at Mark.

Junior grabbed his arm and put it to his father's mouth.

"Come on, daddy." Heidi said to her father, "Take a bite."

Gale's jaw opened and then closed down on

Mark's exposed arm. The old man's false teeth moved in his mouth and then slipped out. Mark screamed as Gale's gums squeezed down on the raw nerves of his muscles and he sucked and drooled on his wounds.

"Get off me, you sick sons a bitches!!" Mark tried to wriggle his way from underneath Heidi.

Heidi laughed and grabbed his other arm and bit down into his forearm. He cried out as she jerked her head back to rip out a chunk. He felt a searing pain from his calf as Junior bit down into his leg and pulled out a wet chunk of skin and meat.

"PLEASE!!!" Mark let out one final cry, but it went unheard as the remaining Kelso's began their orgasmic cannibalistic feast.

Before darkness claimed him, he moaned a tired breath as bits and pieces were tugged away from his limp body.

RUNNING ALONE

This was the very first story I ever wrote. It has bits and pieces of nightmares and the rest is story-telling. I did a fairly drastic overhaul since the first draft, but I did keep the first sentence out of respect to my younger self. The setting is the same as the original as well as the main character and the antagonist....

The Minnesota wind stung his face with a merciless vengeance. Almost feeling like nature was sandblasting his skin from his skull. He had made it as far as Truman, which was a good 60 plus miles from his hometown of St Peter.

He did most of the trip on foot, as his car gave out just on the other side of Mankato. But he knew it wouldn't take long for it to come. It wasn't going let him get far. It wasn't personal, it was just what it did.

He made his way to the dilapidated barn, checking to see if there were any lights on at the adjoining farmhouse. It was quiet, and he thought maybe it had already made its way here. But he was tired, and needed a place in from the rain.

The straw was old and moldy. Dust so thick in threatened to choke him out, it filled his lungs. He quietly coughed to himself and made a nest from the old moldy straw.

As he drifted into a nightmarish sleep he thought about that first night....

He was a bartender at the O'Gara's Pub and Grill. It was a small town pub that sat back away from the main drag. Not many college kids, mostly locals.

Tonight, his regulars sat around in their "assigned" seats. Drinking the same drinks, bitching about the same ills that have been bugging them since he began slinging spirits 6 years ago.

Two seats sat empty at the center of the bar. Usually the barstools were filled by a Vernon Henderson and Larry Winthrop. There was something that made Kyle feel uneasy about his two biggest ass pains being absent tonight. They were both single men. They worked as welders at Gephardt's from 9 in the morning to 5 p.m. Monday through Friday; and every single one of those days they would be sitting in those seats by 5:30 p.m. and wouldn't leave them until Kyle kicked them out at 1:30 a.m. It was Thursday.

"Hey, Kyle." Tommy Gaylord spoke up, "Hey, man, can you turn up the TV? Maybe sling me another whiskey seven while you're at it."

Kyle turned down the stereo and turned up the television and began pouring Tommy another drink. His fifth.

"....cation loss is sporadic which may have to do with the storm front that seems to have engulfed the northern part of the state." Channel 11 weather had a map of the state that had its northern half covered in what looked like a storm front, "Some of the glitches you see on the screen is interference that we've been trying to clear up. The storm seems to be effecting our satellite feed."

The satellite signal to the Twin Cities did seem to be fading in and out most the day, and tonight it was getting worse.

"We've sent out Geoff Hector out on location near Osakis." The weatherman continued, "Geoff how do things look up north?"

The feed was black. It also made Kyle feel uneasy, because the static that came through the newsfeed sounded like a thousand whispering voices.

"We'll get back to Geoff when we can clear up the signal.

"In other news, a large number of animals, both wild and domesticated; have turned up dead across the state. The DNR have been investigating the phenomenon since it started a few weeks a...."

The television picture became drenched in rainbow colors and then went to static. Kyle didn't want to hear that whispering anymore and he shut the television off.

"What the hell was that?" Tommy said laying cash down for his drink.

"The joys of satellite television, Tommy." Kyle said and turned the stereo back up.

"You notice there's been a lot of dead animals lately?"

"The usual road kill. 169 runs right through the center of town, we're likely to get a lot of dead animals from the road."

"Squirrels." Nick Montgomery said, "I usually get half a million squirrels eating up and wrecking my bird feeders. But I've been finding nothing but dead carcasses in my yard. At first I thought it was some of the neighbor kids pickin' them off with their pellet guns. But the damn varmints look like they been dead for weeks. Strangest thing."

"I lost Poncho." Ellie spoke up, "She hadn't come home for a few days. Then when I was raking leaves yesterday, there she was. Just a husk of a body. Like she'd been dead for a long time."

"Okay, guys," Kyle said wiping down the bar. "You guys are getting all X-files on me. You think aliens are mutilating our animals?"

After he said that, he thought about his own dog. A German Shepard that went by the name of "Daisy".

When the clock hit 1:30 a.m. and the last of his customers staggered out the door, Kyle locked the door and then clicked on the television again. Nothing but static. He clicked through the channels and he only got "Loss of signal" message on each channel.

He counted out the register and locked up. He made his night deposit at Wells Fargo and decided to drive his Gran Torino by Vernon's house.

Vernon lived up in the bluffs. It was a two story that he shared with Larry. It sat on 6 acres deep in the woods that overlooked the river. He pulled down their long gravel driveway and around their machine shed where they welded on occasion for some side work.

Both their cars were in front of the house. The house stood dark with only the light above their kitchen sink on. He left the car running and walked up to the door and gave it a couple knocks.

Larry and Vern had several dogs, 7 at last count, but none of them barked and he couldn't see any lurking in the dooryard.

"Hey! Vern!" Kyle shouted, "Larry! You guys up? You guys okay?"

There was no answer from the darkness inside. He walked around and peered in the few windows that graced the main floor. The dining room table was set with a decent sized meal for two single men who usually drank their nutrients.

There was a low grumbling roar coming from the clouds above. He looked up to a starless sky and shivered a bit.

He walked around to the back of the house and found the bodies of 6 dogs of various pedigrees. They looked as if they had been dead for months, some were merely skeletons with skin and fur stretched over them.

More rumbling above, but this time he thought he heard voices. Like a thousand whispering voices like in the static he heard on television.

He felt the hair stand up on the back of his neck and he hurried to his car. He pulled off in a hurry, spraying gravel behind him.

Kyle pulled into the Nicolette County Sheriff's department. He spoke to one of the sergeants on duty.

"If you could just do a welfare check on them." Kyle asked, "It looks like they're home, but no one answered the door. Found their dogs dead in the back."

"Kid," Deputy Windom said. "I can have someone check tomorrow. We've got our hands full with other disappearances, AND dead animals. Farmers all over the county are losing their farm animals.

"I'm sure your friends will show up. A couple of town drunks getting lost in the woods while on a bender is not anything new."

Kyle was going to argue with him, but decided the cop had other problems. He'd wait it out and check back later.

His alarm never went off the next morning. He looked at his phone and it was blank and would not turn on. He shook it several times and then checked the charger plugged into the wall. Power outage.

"Great." He thought, *"It's going to be one of those days."*

He sat up and rubbed his eyes and tried to focus in the dark of his bedroom. Daisy sat next to his bed panting as if she were hot.

"What's the matter, girl?" he asked her and she responded with a heavy paw on his arm.

He stood up, slipped his flip flops on and walked to the window. He pulled the blinds and felt disoriented as it was still night out.

"What the fuck?" he said to himself.

Daisy whined and made her way anxiously to the door.

"Hang on, Daisy."

He shuffled his way into the bathroom and took a leak. He pulled his wristwatch off the medicine cabinet and looked at the time: 9:48 a.m.

"Must be really cloudy outside, huh?" he asked his dog who only whined more and scratched at the door.

Grabbing his sweatshirt, he unlocked the door to his small one-bedroom house nestled by the river and walked uneasily out with Daisy.

She took a leak herself with her nose working up in the air.

He looked up himself and felt panic seeing the sky filled with what looked like black smoke. As if a volcano had erupted.

"What do you smell, girl?" he asked.

Having finished her duty, she kicked dead leaves over her mess and began barking at the sky.

"Okay, that's enough."

But she kept at it. Yapping over and over at something in the air. It was beginning to hurt his ears.

"Daisy!" he grabbed the scruff of her neck, "Enough, I said!"

A loud crack came from the sky and then echoed off the bluffs sending Daisy whining to his side.

"What's the matter?" he asked and then turned towards the house, "C'mon, let's go back in."

She wouldn't budge. She sat next to him growling at some invisible foe.

"Fine, bark at the sky all you want, I'm going inside."

She followed him to the door, but sat on the porch and yipped at the sky.

He scrubbed his teeth and then put on some socks and shoes, he decided to head over to St. James Lutheran Church. He was sure his dad would be there working on this coming Sunday's sermon.

Tying the last lace of his sneakers he opened the front door and saw Daisy lying on her side breathing heavily.

"Daisy?" he said kneeling next to her, "What's the matter, gir....!"

She let out a long labored gasped and her body caved in releasing a thin wisp of black smoke from her mouth that spiraled upward to join the rest of the blackness.

"Jesus! Daisy!!" he began to cry. His dog laid there looking like she had died weeks ago.

He picked her up and laid her on the front porch. He got into his car and drove off to his father's church.

Littered along the streets were hundreds of bird carcasses. Crows, ducks, geese, sparrows, robins, and finches. It made his stomach churn to hear the crunching beneath his tires.

"The fuck is happening?" he asked himself.

The church parking lot was empty. Normally, Jenny Clear Lake's Mazda would be parked there. She was a Lakota woman who had been the church secretary long before his dad took over as Pastor. She was so punctual you could set a watch to her.

He walked up the steps but the front doors were locked. He went around to the side door and that was also locked. On the other side of the lot was the parsonage where his parents lived. He looked back at the church and a loud crack echoed out of the depths of those black clouds again.

He sprinted across the parking lot to his parent's house and the door was locked. He pulled his keys out of his pocket and found his copy of his dad's house key. Opening the door, he yelled for his parents.

There was no answer.

The wind picked up outside and he noticed broken glass on the floor all around him. The windows had been blown out sometime in the night.

"Mom!" he shouted, "Dad!!"

He looked all over the main floor and then made his way upstairs to their bedroom. He got to the top of the steps and called for them one more time. He was answered by the heavy winds and loud thunder.

He opened their bedroom door. Both his parents were upright in bed. Naked and staring opposite of each other.

"Mom?" he asked in an unsteady tone, "Dad? Are you guys, okay?"

He approached his mother slowly, picking up the covers which were lying on the floor. He was going to cover his mother's nakedness when he noticed in the dim light that her eyes were black pools of glass.

"*Kyle.*" His father spoke in a monotone voice, but it wasn't just his voice; it was mixed with a chorus of a thousand others, making him jump nonetheless, "*My son, your mother belongs to me now. As does your father and soon....you.*"

"What are you....?" Kyle backed off from his mother.

"*Don't fight it, son.*" His mom said in the same flat tone as his father, "*We can all be together. Just let it happen.*"

His mother pounced on him, catching him off guard and knocking him to the ground. Without any emotion, she pinned him down with her knees and pried his mouth open.

"*He is ready.*" She said still staring straight ahead, "*He's ready to join us.*"

"Mom!" Kyle screamed, "Get the fuck off me!!"

She was a heavy set woman. But the thought of his mother's naked body atop his and the strange and horrifying situation that was happening before him pumped him full of adrenaline. He was able to get his right arm free and as he struggled to get the rest of himself free his father stood above him, grabbing his free arm.

"Dad! Please, fight this! Where's your faith? Why are you doing this??"

His father laughed, "*Silly boy. Faith has nothing to do with me. I am a simple entity, hungry for the essence you humans carry within you.*"

Pastor Henry Scott knelt at his son's head while his wife of 27 years pried open Kyle's mouth. As his father bent down opening his mouth towards his own, Kyle felt his life draining from himself. Gagging and tearing up, he saw a new blackness in the already dark room.

Then, in one fleeting moment, clarity returned to him. The dimness became lighter, and when his focus came back, his father fell to the floor. Before he knew what was happening, he heard a loud crack and then his mother fell to the right of him.

Someone grabbed him from behind and struggled with lifting him to his feet.

"Who the fuck?" he uttered looking behind him.

"Easy." Jenny Clear Lake spoke to him, "We must return to the chapel immediately!"

"Jenny! My God, what's happening? What happened to my parents?"

"Something that can't be undone. But we must get back to the chapel, it is not safe here!"

They both ran down the steps and into the chapel, locking the doors behind them. Jenny had a bundle of sage smoldering on the altar of his father's church. She grabbed it and began smudging the area around Kyle. The scent made his lungs tight but he let her finish. She then ran to the entrance to the worship center and smudged that as well and left a trail of sea salt she had in a leather medicine bag across the entryway.

"Please, Jenny." He asked, "Tell me what's happening? What's wrong with my parents? What's happening out there?"

"Something evil has escaped the great abyss." She said solemnly, "It is ancient, and claiming the land that it once ruled."

"I....I don't understand."

"You can't. You were raised on your father's God. The white man's legends. But my grandfather was one of the great elders who passed on the ancient tales to me."

"But...that...that thing...it spoke through my dad's voice and said that...that faith has nothing to do with it....?"

"The Christian bible, your bible, tells tales of the ancient spirits and demons of the Hebrews...and the Hebrew lands. This land...MY people's land...we had our own spirits and demons. Our own legends that we battled when mankind was young."

Kyle tried to grasp what she was saying. Above, thunder clapped in the sky sounding like a large sledgehammer being pounded on the roof.

"What are we going to do?" He asked, "What can we do?"

Jenny continued to smudge around the altar, "I'm afraid I don't know."

"What?"

"I was taught to heal people spiritually, physically, emotionally…even to protect against negative energies. But this…this is far bigger than anything I am prepared to handle."

Thunder smashed the glass and busted open the doors of the sanctuary. The black cloud filled the borders of the entryway while Jenny grabbed Kyle's arm and led him to the altar.

"Hold fast to your beliefs, young man, whatever they are!" She said to him.

She reached into her medicine bag and tossed out a powder at the blackness. Little flashes of lightning erupted inside the mass. She held out her sage smudge stick fanning the thick smoke with a large decorated eagle feather.

"You are not welcome here, ancient one! We are protected by the white light! We are protected by our ancestors!"

A wisp of black cloud shot out like a tendril and snuffed out the burning sage. Jenny snapped her hand back that began smoldering with frost.

Your petty magicks will not work on me, It hissed in that horrid hollow chorus. *Your ancestors fed me. You, will feed me. I will take what is mine.*

Jenny grabbed her medicine bag and threw the entire satchel into the cloud. The flashes of lightning were brighter and it seemed to corrupt the blackness. It began to dissipate and retreat back outside.

Jenny collapsed to her knees.

"I think you did it!" Kyle said rushing to her side, "Are you okay?"

"We...." Jenny sounded exhausted, "We should leave....I don't think I will survive another attack like that."

He helped her up and they made their way to the entrance. He stopped dead in his tracks when he heard the whispering again. Surrounding him on either side.

"Jenny?" he spoke softly, "Can you hear that?"

She didn't answer.

Blackness spilled back into the sanctuary, this time slithering around Jenny. Kyle snapped his arm back as the shadowy mist began to freeze his arm and numb it.

"Jenny!!" He yelled to her.

"Kyle!" she whimpered, "Kyle, save meeeeeeeeeeeeeeee........!"

The blackness engulfed her and she disappeared into the obsidian fog. He ran to the altar and grabbed the large iron cross that sat atop the wooden altar and held it in front of him.

Oh, you are such a funny man-child. It teased, *Do you think your objects are going to help you?*

Another black wisp of cloud wrapped around the metal cross. Kyle felt the intense cold running down the brass handle. He used as much will as he could to hold onto it, but his hands went numb and it began to feel like a white hot burn.

He released the crucifix, leaving layers of skin on it. The black tendrils held it in the air above him and then crushed it into a perfect sphere.

"Oh, shit!" he cussed.

The sphere flew through the air towards him and he dived to the side as it smashed through the raised altar. Splinters of wood stabbed into his side as he screamed out.

Enough playing around, Kyle. There was impatience in its voice, *Come to me. Come to me now so that I may devour you.*

"Leave!" Kyle screamed, "This cannot be real!! Just leave me alone!"

A black tendril coiled around his ankle and dragged him closer. He protested but the coldness of its touch began to sap the fight out of him.

Soooooo, delicious. Not as delectable as your father...but delightful just the same!

"NO!!" Kyle grabbed ahold of a pew and held steadfast, "NO!! I will NOT go!!"

The cold ate into his ankle and ran up his leg to his groin. He reached into the pew and caught hold of a copy of the bible and threw it into the dark. A large blue light exploded inside it and it released him. Pins and needles ran up and down his legs as he tried to stand.

"My faith may not kill you!" He spat, "But it can hurt you!!"

The inky darkness boiled at the entrance, loud thunder echoed from its depths into the large chapel. Then, it simply sucked itself out of the church and into the air, leaving 3 naked figures standing at the entryway. It was his parents and Jenny. A faint grey mist danced around their bodies. Their eyes were black mirrors.

"My son." The dad thing spoke.

"Stop!" Kyle grabbed a candelabra from the aisle. A set up for a wedding this Saturday, "I am NOT your son! You are no longer my father!"

"The truth is a painful thing to grasp, Kyle. But we are all here as cattle. We always have been."

"Those are lies!!" Kyle swings the candelabra at Jenny who was closest to him and approaching fast, "Your time is OVER!"

A low guttural laugh erupted from the depths of the ghastly trio.

"Your father is right." The Jenny-thing spoke, *"our ancestors were put here as food. It hibernates for millions of years*

and awakens to feed. It is a natural cycle. It only seems unnatural because it doesn't happen often."

"Join us." His mother added, *"It is inevitable."*

It was his father, who tried to grab at him first. With heavy regret on his heart he swung the candelabra and connected with his father's head bringing the good pastor to the ground. Kyle brought the long metal rod back to crash it into what used to be his father's face when Jenny tackled him down and climbed upon him.

"Get off me!" he yelled, "I will not join you!"

She pried his mouth open and lowered her face to his. Feeling his life being sucked out of him again, he pulled a long sliver that was embedded in his waist and jabbed it deep into Jenny's eye. It popped in a thick black goo that spattered his face.

He threw her off as he stood up. His mother came from behind and bit down into the wound where the splintered wood was in his waist and began sucking away at it.

"GODDAMMIT!!" he screamed and tried to elbow her in the face, "Get the fuck off me!!"

But she only continued to feed greedily at him. He grabbed his mother's face and dug into her eye sockets with his thumbs.

More of the same black ichor splattered his grimacing face. She let go and dropped to the floor.

He stumbled out the front of the church and made his way to his car. Screams could be heard from all over St. Peter. Police sirens wailed and then would die. Ambulance and other emergency vehicles would rise and die in the distance.

As he made his way to 169, which ran through the center of town following the river, he decided to head south. The news reports had said it was coming from the north, so his only choice was south.

The drive between St. Peter and Mankato is one of the most beautiful scenic rides one can take any time of the year in Minnesota. But today, it was pitch black; not even with his headlights on "high" could he penetrate the darkness. The only thing he could see was dead bodies of people and animals strewn about the roads and sidewalks. Hanging out of their broken down cars were husks of what was once human.

"This is silly, Kyle." It spoke through his car radio, *"You cannot run from your destiny."*

He shut the radio off. Then his car began to sputter and then shut off. It drifted to the bottom of the hill coasting into the lot of a Happy Chef parking lot.

"Son of a bitch!" Kyle spat as he pounded on the steering wheel.

When the car came to a stop he got out and looked around. He would glance nervously up at the sky as distant thunder clapped in the distance off to the north.

He awoke in the moldy straw. He could feel eyes looking at him. He scanned the darkness and saw a dark figure standing several feet away from him. He backed slowly away from it.

"You move one more inch, boy, and I'll put two holes in you with both barrels." Spoke the man in the shadows.

"You're....alive?" Kyle said putting his trembling hands in the air.

"Of course I'm alive!" the man said, "You on drugs?"

"No...no I...I'm sorry, I just needed shelter from the rain. I don't mean any harm."

"You're lucky it was me and not my missus! She spooks easy." The man laughs, and it is an old man's laugh.

Kyle only nervously chuckles and lowers his hands slowly.

"I'd turn the lights on in the barn but the power went out this morning. That damn storm comin' outta the north. Weirdest thing is it even drained all the damn batteries around here too."

"It's not the storm."

"Solar flare type thing, ya think?"

"No."

"Well, in any case, my name's Elmer Newport. You're welcome to come in and get warm. Got the wood stove goin' and I can have Betty put some coffee on."

"Kyle." He put out his hand.

"Don't be scared, young man, I ain't gonna shoot ya." Elmer said pumping Kyle's hand.

Elmer led him up to the house. Thunder crashed above them and Kyle almost urinated himself.

"Man, you're jumpy." Elmer commented, "Where did you say you're from?"

"I didn't." Kyle answered nervously, "But I'm from St. Peter."

"You walked all this way?"

"From Mankato, yes."

Elmer shook his head and opened the front door for him. Kyle stepped in and the old farmer came in behind him.

"Betty!" Elmer hollered, "Betty, I've brought in a guest! Got some coffee on?"

"How nice." She said from the other room, *"Invite him in, invite him in!"*

Kyle stopped dead in his tracks. He thought he had heard several voices within the old lady's voice.

"The hell is wrong with you, Kyle?" Elmer asked, "C'mon in."

"I....I can't...I....."

"Betty, can you come out here and give me a hand?"

"No! Please, we must get out!" Kyle grabbed his arm, "We have to go, that's not your wife!"

"Not my…? You better leave, buddy!" Elmer's face got grim, "I ain't harboring no weirdos! You from that mental institution in St. Peter? That where you from?"

"Seriously, sir! You need to go! We both need to go!"

Elmer raised his double barrels at Kyle and cocked the hammers back, "You better get out of my home RIGHT fuckin' now, boy! I ain't kiddin! Betty! You stay in the kitchen!"

But Betty had other plans. She came out into the mud room from behind Elmer. Her eyes black as shiny coal.

"Lighten up, Elmer." She said with a thousand whispering voices, *"And give mama a kiss!"*

To Kyle's horror, (or more likely to Elmer's as well), Betty pushed her husband against the wall and pressed her lips to his. The shotgun went off and blew two holes in the door behind Kyle. There were sucking sounds and then Elmer began to gag, as if his breath was being sucked from his lungs. His arms flailed as his life left him, and he eventually just curled into an empty heap.

Kyle had grabbed ahold of the shotgun. He was pointing it at Betty repeatedly pulling the trigger. It only clicked and clicked with both barrels already empty.

"Relax, Kyle." The Betty thing said wiping her mouth, *"I've decided not to eat you. You want to live out your self-righteous existence while the rest of your kind gets fed upon, so be it."*

"I don't believe you." Kyle said backing towards the door.

"There are billions of souls on this planet, Kyle. Not eating you is not going disturb me. I've decided it would be more delectable to let you live through this. Live through the near extinction of your race."

"NEAR extinction?"

"It wouldn't be very prudent of me to wipe out my food supply. I'll have to leave some of you around after I hibernate. Repopulate the food supply. It will be interesting to see what you evolve into in a few million years. See what kind of religion you come up with."

"Someone will stop you! Someone will destroy you for good!"

"I am eternal! You are a fool to think that this world...that this universe was made for YOU! It may not even be made for me!

Maybe the next time I wake there will be something bigger around to digest me? I highly doubt that, but anything is possible.

"Anyways, enjoy your pardon, food. I've got a world to feed to on."

Kyle stepped down off the front steps. He backed his way towards the barn and curled into the fetal position in his moldy straw nest. He put his thumb into his mouth and tried to find a happy place in his mind.

THE DIARY OF KATHRYN EMERSON

This was originally going to be a prequel to my zombie novel Zechariah 14: 12-humanity's last stand. *After researching for that story I found that the source material is so ungodly large that it needs to be its own novel; which will be titled* Jeremiah 19:9-in the beginning. *So then I was tasked with writing a SEQUEL, and I didn't know how to tell it. So I reread Zechariah (okay, the last chapter) and decided that this was going to be told by our former hero's youngest daughter Kathryn, who barely had a voice in the first book....*

April 24th Hillmont Island, MN

So today is my 14th birthday. We didn't celebrate my birthday the last two years because we've been too busy trying to survive. If this were a perfect world, and things were like they used to be; Mom and dad would have the picnic shelter rented out on Gibbous Lake in my hometown of Fair Lakes. All my friends would be there playing games, swimming, talking about boys. Dad would be grilling those delicious "Len burgers" and mom would be setting up the piñata. Our dog Jack would be chasing us around the park with a large stick in his mouth. We'd eat and then open presents. Nana would be snapping photos like a maniac and telling me to open her present first. We'd eat cake with a photo of Justin Bieber in the frosting, and we'd end up having a big cake fight giving dad a heart attack.

But that was before the RAC-V hit the world. Turning our world into something like out of the horror movies dad used to watch with me. He's gone now. Hank Doble had to shoot him in the head. Mom said he was infected. I don't know if I believe that. He was the strongest man I know and knew how to get out of any problem that life threw at him. It is because of dad that my sister Leigh and I made it through the beginning of the outbreak. Nana is gone too. I had to watch her kill herself with a knife because she got bit.

Only Leigh, mom and myself now. Hank got us here, to a new safety zone. We rode in a tank. The President ordered nuclear weapons to be dropped on a handful of big cities to help the military fight the "deadheads". Airstrikes of napalm were dropped throughout the country as a secondary wave.

When we got to Goose Lake, we had to swim to Hillmont Island. We've been here ever since. It is a safe zone. I feel more secure here than I did at the Moon Valley County Fairgrounds in Fair Lakes. There are high fences around the island. Shelters were built up in the trees. It was crowded, and in the beginning they had to weed out the sick. It was a scary time. Seeing families being ripped apart as their infected loved ones were "euthanized".

Mom, being a nurse, was busy most of the time helping the injured. Having the most medical training, she was also in charge of what she called "triage". It's her decision who gets euthanized and who gets treated.

That left my sister and I to fend for ourselves most the time. Leigh can be bossy most of the time and a know-it-all, but since we lost our dad; she's been pretty mellow.

There hasn't been any danger from the dead heads. They apparently can't swim. The only danger falls on the scouts who go to the mainland to search for supplies. I am too young to scout, so I get to stay here and help with cooking or taking care of the younger ones. Not really a thrill for me, but there are no Xboxes anymore. No ipods or ipads. No internet, as far as I know. But really, I think there has to be, because no one really mans the internet...it's just floating out there in the air, right? Hmmmm.....

Anyhow, even though I didn't expect a party, mom got me something for my birthday. She must have got it from one of the scouts, but here it is. This notebook. I know it doesn't sound like much but I've been dying to journal or something since everything went south. So here it is: my first journal entry. And maybe, just maybe, this is going to be the only written record of the "zombie apocalypse". (ugh, sounds so cheesy calling it that!)

Leigh went even further for my birthday. She's a scout now. Has been since her 16th birthday. I was scared for her. She doesn't cope well with stress. Even less since dad died. He was always her rock. But she came back after her first outing. She was changed a bit. Maybe not so much for the good though. She would always talk to me before. About anything. It was somewhat annoying. But now, she hardly says anything. It makes me sad to see her so….hard…like this. But she must have found basic ingredients to make a cake last time she was out. Because this morning, she baked me a cake. Just a plain jane cake, with honey for frosting, but the smell was so intoxicating!!

Some of the other survivors smelled the cake and came over wanting some. I was going to share but Leigh lost her shit on them. Told them to "back the fuck off" me. Doble had come to calm her down and she broke into tears and ran into our tree hut.

Mr. Doble gave me the weirdest gift, but I think it is one of my favorite treasures. He pulled out a blue bandana from his shirt pocket. There was dried blood stains on it and I almost thought it was going to be some freak body part from one of the dead heads. (I really did). But he told me that it was my father's.

That dad had used it as a tourniquet during the fall of the Moon Valley Fairgrounds. He said my dad's tears were also dried in this bandana. He kept the bandana because he said from Viet Nam to the oil fields of Kuwait, he had never served with a better man than my dad.

It made me cry. Because even though it had been in Mr. Doble's pocket all this time, it had a faint hint of dad's scent in it. His face still burns in my memories. To think about what dad went through just to get to us at nana's farm and then to find mom and keep us safe at the same time. Just to end up getting infected anyways and being shot in the head by your best friend.

I think I need to walk away from all this writing for a while.....

April 30th.

Wow! I get all excited about a stupid notebook and say I'm going to write in it every day and I blow off a week!

I'm worried about my sister. She's become very aggressive, not towards me but towards mom and everyone else. Mom said she's probably going through something called PTSD. I don't know exactly what that means, but mom said it's kind of like going nuts because you've seen too many "bad" things happen.

Well, haven't all of us? Leigh has always been pretty sensitive, but I've never seen her get angry like she does. This boy named Carlos used to come around a lot wanting to talk to her. He was always really nice to everyone, and they seemed to have a good time together but the last time he came up to our hut she put her gun in his face and told him if he ever came around her again she'd "Shoot his fuckin' nuts off" and laugh as he bled out.....wow....wtf?

There are no boys here my age. They are all either wayyyyy older or wayyyyyy younger. There are no girls here my age for that matter. Blah.

I like to listen to the stories the scouts talk about when they come back. They usually sit up all night bragging about their adventures around a campfire. Sometimes, I'm jealous of

Leigh. Being able to go out there, off the island. I don't even know what's going on out there. For all I know, the scouts are lying and everything is back to normal.

I better go, mom and Leigh are in another screaming match....

May 2nd.

Mother's day. I can't even go shopping for her. I can hear dad's voice in the back of my head "Kathryn! Even making a card for her, making her a little dinner, or something, anything....just show her you appreciate her!"

So I had Mr. Doble take me outside the fence and we went fishing off the beach this morning. If mom knew I was outside the fence she'd have a fit, but seeing that I was catching these fish to fry up for mom, Mr. Doble helped me out.

We caught 4 sunfish, a good size bass, and 3 crappies. I didn't know how to fillet or fry them up, but he showed me how. It was actually pretty interesting and the aroma of fish frying over a fire was such a treat.

I threw in a couple potatoes and now, I'm going to bring them to mom at our makeshift hospital. Wish me luck! ☺

May 4th.

Ugh. I don't even know how to start this.…My mother, who I'm going to call by her name now…"Kris"…is a SLUT!!!

There. I said it. I fucking said it.

On mother's day, when Leigh and I went to give Kris her dinner and a card we both made, at the hospital...she wasn't even there. She was with one of the scouts named Nick. It was mother's day, and she told us she would be working. But she was with him. How many nights when she could have been hanging out with us was she with him when she should have been at work??? And daddy died! Trying to save her, save us!! I hate her I really fucking HATE HER!!!

Leigh took it the worst. She attacked Kris. Then she attacked that Nick guy. It was intense! I thought she was going to kill him.

Leigh told Kris never to come back to our hut again. And I really don't care if she ever does. But she did follow us back to the hut. Leigh latched the metal door at the top of the ladder so she couldn't come up. She banged away at the door and hollered up to let her up, but we both went into our hut and ignored her. She eventually left. Probably back to her fuck buddy.

I did feel a little bad. It's hard for her to climb the ladder with her bad leg. The one she cut off because the RAC-V was slithering around inside it. But, then I thought...she has no problem climbing Nick's ladder does she?

May 7th.

Kris is living "at the hospital", or so she says. But Leigh has been watching. She spends most her time in the hospital, but she's been sleeping at Nick's.

It's okay. We've been fending for ourselves most of the time anyways. She's been too busy at the hospital to give a shit about us. Besides, dad taught us how to survive. He taught us to be brave. We don't need her.

Maybe we should go easy on her. Times have been rough on everybody. It has been two years since dad was killed. She should be able to move on. I guess I'm mad at her because she didn't tell us. It's like she lied to us. Telling us she was working when really she was doing things with this Nick guy.

I'm worried about tomorrow. It's another scouting mission and its Leigh's turn to go out. I've never been completely alone before. I'm not afraid of the dead heads. I more afraid of the others who live here. I don't know most of them. Some of them look shady. Some of them look at me weird. Plus, knowing mom ordered some of their infected loved ones to death...well...I've heard whispers...

May 8th.

It's night. Leigh is gone. Her boat left at 8 this morning. I've done village chores most the day, but dinner and now...alone.

I locked the door to the ladder so no one can get up here. Just in time too, because they came. A group of about 20. They had baseball bats, some even had knives, and they were calling up to me. Calling me names. Telling me that since my mom had their family killed they were going to kill her family.

They're banging away at the hatch leading to the catwalk to our tree hut. I tried to stay quiet but I couldn't. I thought that they were going to make it up here to me. What am I going to do? Leigh had all the guns. I didn't even have a knife!

I wish mom was here!

I wish dad was here!

I wish Mr. Doble was here!

They're shouting that they're going to burn the trees down if I won't come out. Where's my mom? Oh my god, they're throwing torches up here! I have to go! I have to get rid of these torches before they

May 10th.

They killed her. They killed my mom. She ran to the hut to see what all the noise was about up here and someone impaled her with a spear. The crowd got ravenous and just....

They ripped her apart. Literally. They tore her limb from limb.

When they finished they looked up at me and smiled. They fucking smiled at me. My mother laid there below our hut in pieces. They fucking smiled at me!

Leigh should be here soon. They only do 24hr missions. She'll be here and Mr. Doble will be here and then there will be some fucking justice! I'm sure mom's fuck buddy Nick won't be all too happy either when he gets back! Fuckers!

I'm sorry mom.....I'm sorry you died like that...I'm sorry we were so mean to you.....

May 11th.

They're not back yet! Something's wrong. Something happened.

May 12th.

Still nothing. I won't leave the hut. I can't. Mom is still down there. In pieces. She's beginning to smell. I've got food and water. I hope Leigh comes back soon. I'm scared.

May 13th.

The camp is quiet. The scouts aren't back yet. I can only think the worst has happened. The smell is horrible. I had use a bucket to go to the bathroom and I dumped it over the railings. That mixed with the smell of mom rotting out there is unbearable.

Where the fuck are you Leigh?????

May 14th.

I tried to sneak down last night. I was going to climb the fence and take a boat to the mainland and try to find everybody. But as I got to the top of the fence I saw three boats. I thought it was Leigh and the rest of the scouts. But the lead boat stopped just short of the shoreline and dropped a group of about 15 dead heads. I came back down and watched as they shambled their way to the shore.

They started banging against the fence. It alerted one of the guards and people started waking up and coming to the fence. I hid in the bushes watching as the boats went around to the other side of the island.

Our people started jabbing at the infected with spears and killing a few of them. I had almost forgotten what those things looked and smelled like. It was horrible.

Since there were less human beings around the dead heads were beginning to liquefy from lack of food. They moved slower. Mr. Doble said he heard reports about the dead heads, and how the RAC-V virus fed on its host which is why the infected had to feed on living tissue to survive; If the infected didn't get food, then their bodies started to break down as the virus devoured its host.

While the people were busy I ran back here to the safety of my hut. But I still wonder where those boats were going. Why would they drop off a boat load of dead heads here?

May 15th.

Gunshots. Screaming. Then silence. I don't know what's happening down there but I'm going to stay hidden.

May 20th.

They were another group. Mostly young. They looked like they would have been in high school when the outbreak happened. Now, they're just teens in adult bodies.

They took over our island. They released the dead heads to see what kind of weapons we had. There were only a few guns held by the guards. They were killed first. The rest of us had primitive melee weapons. But they had all kinds of guns and we quickly surrendered.

They killed our weak. Most of the group that killed my mother were dead. Some of them lived, and I made sure to keep my eyes out for them.

Most of us, me included, gave up on our scouts ever coming back.

I am truly alone now...

I am able to keep the hut, but they took all my food and water. They keep all our supplies in the larger hut which their leader stays in with his girlfriend. They ration our supplies to us depending on the work we do. Really, it depends on what mood they're in.

I still do the community cooking. Help in the garden. Watch the kids. There is no more hospital. The new people killed everyone who was sick or wounded and put them in a boat, soaked them in what was left of our kerosene, and lit them on fire and sent them out on the water.

June 3rd.

Tonight one of those new boys came up to the hut. It was late. He tried to put his hands on me. He held me down and kissed me, but I didn't kiss him back. I bit his cheek and scratched his eyes. Leigh taught me that.

I know I'll probably pay for that tomorrow....

June 4th.

So they made me a soldier. It's their version of a scout. The leader was impressed how I handled myself with Pete. Said that ferocity like mine was being wasted over the stove and in the garden and I should be out getting supplies.

I'm not sure if that's a promotion or a punishment. But if I can get on the mainland, I can look for Leigh.

It worries me that there are still dead heads around though. I thought they'd mostly be gone since all the bombing and lack of food. But I guess that would make them more desperate too. The ones they dropped here looked horrible.

They gave me a gun. A 1911. Two clips of ammo and they sent me out on the beach to target shoot with one of the other guys. His name was Kent. Typical douche bag jock. Pompous, full of himself, and thought I was ga-ga over him because he was god's gift. YUCK!

Thought I'd play my cards right. Pretended to be the stupid shallow female he thought I was. Pretended I didn't know how to handle a gun. I was just a hopeless damsel in distress.

He told me I'd be ready for a supply run in two days.

June 6th.

Early AM. I'm ready. Nervous as hell, but ready. I have the gun they gave me, a knife, and I was given 32 rounds for the 9mm. Heading to the boat in a sec, just wanted to write this down because it all seems so surreal. I read back a few entries and things have changed so dramatically so quickly. And we just accepted it, adapt, and move on like its normal. Is it? I'm bringing the notebook with, write more tonight.

Late PM. Talcot, MN. They stuck me in a group with the four remaining people who killed my mother. The only one from the new group was our leader Ken. They were watching me and I was watching them. I knew I was going to end these fuckers that took my family from me before this mission ended.

They had trucks hidden in the bushes on the mainland. We rode into a town called Talcot. There isn't much here. Just a convenience store, a grain elevator and a bar. There were bodies littered everywhere, but they were long dead. I was looking for Leigh or anyone else from our scouting party, but they weren't around.

We went through all the buildings on Main Street. Homes and businesses. Going through the houses was sad. Looking at people's lives that lived here. Family photos, clothes, letters....you know I can't even remember what my house looked like, or even my old bedroom. I remember bits and pieces of our swing set, pieces of furniture, but not my room. Or the rooms that housed the furniture. I remember some of my old toys, my stuffed animals.

We loaded the trucks as we gathered supplies. No dead heads. No other humans.

We moved out into the country, to the farms. Fields were overgrown with grass and some of the corn came back in splotchy patches.

I walked out into the field to pick some of that corn and that's when I ran into a group of dead heads. They surprised me. I had forgot that they go into a sort of dormant state when there isn't food around. They started coming at me from everywhere. I didn't scream. I shot 5 of them square in the forehead. I tripped over some tall grass my foot had gotten tangled in and the gun fell from my hand.

My skin crawled as I heard their desperate gurgling cries, hungry for the meal I brought to them. It grew louder as they gathered around me! I was searching for my gun while trying to get to my feet.

A skeletal hand grabbed my upper arm and the sharp bony fingers dug into my shirt trying to pierce my skin. Bullets ripped past me and shattered the dead head's skull. More bullets whizzed past me, cutting through the tall grass and puncturing the faces and heads of the growing crowd of infected.

I ran out of there onto the gravel driveway of the farm. Those things were crawling out of corn as my group was shooting furiously at the undead crowd. My gun, sitting somewhere in the corn field.

Ken told us to save our ammo and make a break for the house. I told him we'd be better off in the barn. It had a loft and those things couldn't climb. I remembered that from when nana, Leigh and I had to escape at Nana's house.

Ken ran into the house anyways. He brought 3 of our group with him. 2 came with me. They were the ones that were with the group that ripped apart my mother.

So here we are. Still in the barn. We are up in the hay loft. The dead heads got through the barn door pretty easy. It was old rotted wood and their sheer weight splintered it. But they can't get to us.

Well, somehow I've got to sleep. Between listening to those grotesque snarls down there and knowing that the people who brutally murdered my mother are lying near me. I'll get through this. I'll get my revenge. I'll get out of this mess. But I need sleep. Something I haven't been able to do in awhile....

June 8*th*.

I did it. I was able to take one of their guns while they slept and I shot both of them in the lower back. Shattered their spine from the waist down. It made it easy to push them from the loft. I stood there for a brief moment and watched them get torn apart like they tore apart my mother.

But it didn't feel good. To know I ended two lives. I could have just shot them in the head and made it quick. But I didn't. I didn't on purpose. Maybe, it was this type of thing that messed up Leigh. Maybe, Leigh saw that we...mankind...were becoming more brutal than those infected things down there.

Including us. Instead of working together we were working against each other. Stealing...raping...killing one another. We were becoming animals.

I thought about that for a long time after that. It made me cry. What would my dad think about what Leigh and I had become? I'm sorry, daddy, I'm sorry that this is what we've become....like everyone else.

While those dead heads were chewing up those bastards, I decided it would be a good time to make a break for it. There was a small window in the hay loft that looked out onto a slanted tin roof that went down into a pasture. I went out the window and stood on the tin roof to check things out.

The area was clear, nothing around the house either, so I was thinking that Ken and his group were okay. I went inside and seen that they hadn't even looted the place yet. I grabbed a large plastic garbage bag out of the kitchen and began putting food into it. There was a .22 lever action rifle above the kitchen doorway and I strapped that around my shoulder. There was a box of shells in the kitchen drawer but only 18 rounds, better than nothing.

June 9th.

I camped out in the house. I reinforced the doors and I slept upstairs. That gave me the tactical advantage, as dad would say. I'd be able to nail those things before they were able to get up the steps, they'd hog pile and block the doorway for other...things.

I'm a little concerned because I haven't heard or seen any sign of Ken and his group. Did they make a break for the truck? Why didn't they check on us? That would have been awkward since I killed my group, but still.

Random dead heads creep around the dooryard, but the pack has thinned. I feel pretty secure in here. It reminds me of the old pioneer farmhouse we hid out in with dad. I may just make a home of this place. I've got plenty of food. I've got guns. Plenty of things around here I could make into weapons. It's hard not to get cocky, but I made it this far on my own.

June 10*th*.

I saw a campfire last night. Way out in the middle of the corn field. I found a pair of binoculars and tried to zoom in on the camp, but the tall corn and weeds messed up my line of sight. Tomorrow, I'm going to get out there somehow.

June 11*th*.

I found her! Leigh...and Mr. Doble. It wasn't easy getting to them. I had to kill a few of the dead heads. I got lost in that maze of corn, and Leigh almost blew my head off. But instead of shooting me, she hugged me. So did Mr. Doble.

I told them everything that happened. From mom getting killed, to the island being taken over. I thought Leigh was going explode, but she didn't. She just plopped on the ground and wept. I don't think I ever saw her cry that hard before. I comforted her the best I could. When everything got calm again, I asked her what happened to them.

They said they were ambushed by the same crew that took the island. Killed almost everyone in the scouts, including Nick. Leigh and Mr. Doble ran and hid in the corn. When our group came, Leigh noticed they were the same group that attacked them earlier, so they ambushed them when they got to the house running from the horde of dead heads. I said I was almost a part of that group but decided to take the barn instead.

They followed me back to the farmhouse and we ate a nice dinner. Doble said he was going to check around the sheds and see if he could find something for us to drive out of here. I told him there was a truck parked at the end of the drive, but he said that he and Leigh sabotaged it.

Leigh went upstairs to take a well-deserved nap. I used the opportunity to write this down.

June 12th.

Doble said there was a John Deere combine in one of the far machine sheds. It was fueled up and he thought he'd be able to start it. I asked him if he could even drive the thing and he told me he grew up on a farm.

Lived on that same farm and raised his own family there. I was going to ask him where his family was, but judging by the look in his eyes when he talked about them; I didn't really want to know what happened to them.

Food is getting low, and between all 3 of us, we don't have enough ammo to get through another horde or some other group of bandits. It only made sense to head north. We are going to pack up and head out in the morning.

June 13th. Jeffers, MN

We made it to a rock quarry near Jeffers, MN. Not without trouble though. We ran into a horde of dead heads just south of Storden, MN. We had taken the fields most the way. We came into a corn field and ran through several dead heads, which grinded up easily in the combine. But there were a lot of them, and they eventually began to clog up the head and the thresher.

I was riding on the outside, picking off any that tried climbing up while Leigh and Doble tried freeing up the parts. The hard part was getting the head clean out. Doble went down there to clean them off while Leigh and I covered him. But we were only watching the outer perimeter. We weren't watching the actual head where he was at. So because of us, Mr. Doble got bit. It was a half dead head, it had been sheared in half by the blades of the combine, but it was still "alive" and crawling around under the head. It made its way to his leg and before we knew it was on him, it had climbed up halfway up his body and bit down into his back before he was able to knife it in the skull.

Having cleared the combine, and patching Mr. Doble up, we went forward until we reached this quarry. It was perfect. It had a central station up on stilts in the middle of a pond. Conveyors ran in different directions stretching several feet to other minor stations. There were ladders to climb on each one.

We drove the combine into the pond and up to the central station and unpacked all we had. The central station had only one entrance, and a metal door. There was a stairway that spiraled up to a catwalk that went along the windows 360 degrees with an outdoor catwalk as well accessible by a small hatch.

Mr. Doble told us that he wouldn't be joining us in here. I know I wasn't very keen on the idea and Leigh began to cry because he was like a dad to her. But he was infected, and he knew it would be a matter of time before the virus took over his brain and he would be a danger to us. So he took a knife and said he was going to take the combine into town and try and find supplies. He said it may be his last scouting trip. He said he may not be back if the virus takes him.

He hugged us both. Gave us a kiss on our foreheads. And left.

Leigh went up on the catwalk and outside to watch him go. I curled up on my makeshift bed and wrote this.

June 14th.

Doble came back late last night. We went down to greet him and he looked like hell. The veins in his neck were turning black and his skin was getting ashy blue. He was coughing a lot and it sounded wet inside his lungs.

In a low raspy voice, he said that the city of Jeffers was overrun with dead heads. But they didn't bother him because they could smell the virus in him. He had quite the load of supplies with him. More than a months' worth of food, charcoal, lighters, flash lights, batteries, bottled water, pens, notebooks, playing cards, board games, rifles, pistols, ammo, knives, bows, arrows, fishing poles, candles, kerosene, lanterns, and clothes. Clean clothes that were roughly mine and Leigh's size.

We tried to help him out, but he stopped us. He said that he was getting sicker and it was going to turn him soon. He said he could feel it moving around in his head. I shivered at the thought of that. He said he was going to sleep in the cab of the combine.

Checked on him this morning and he was gone. There was a puddle of black goo on the deck of the combine but the cab was empty. Somewhere in the depths of that pond, Hank Doble was "walking".

Leigh and I went inside.

We went out on the catwalk and decided to check out the other stations along the conveyors. It amazed me how far the conveyors reached and the complex system they used to deliver sand and gravel from one end to the other. Looking around it seemed as if we were in a desert.

The northeast station had a dead head in it, but it was barely alive. It was so far gone that it was mostly just a skeleton with skin stretched across in certain parts. When it saw us it growled and tried to reach for us with its muscle deprived arm.

I said we should kill it. Put it out of its misery. Leigh said "no". That it wasn't up to us to decide the fate of one of those things. What a strange thing to say...

July 4th.

I know it's been awhile since I've written. And this will be the last entry. The very last.

Leigh is gone.

She's dead.

We were going to try and dredge the pond for Mr. Doble so that we had a place to bathe. But when Leigh stepped down off the ladder and onto the roof of the combine, she slipped. It had been raining and the roof was wet. She slipped and fell into the pond. I jumped down a bit more carefully but rushed to pull her out. She had ahold of the railing on the deck, but he got her. She gripped onto my arm and I tried to pull her free. But Mr. Doble bit deep into her shoulder. She screamed in pain. I pulled even harder, and he took another chunk out of her. She pleaded with me not to let go and for the love of god I tried not to. I tried, I honestly tried. But he kept eating her, and soon her grip began to loosen. But those beautiful deep brown eyes of hers just stared a hole into me.

I'm so sorry, sis. I'm so fucking sorry. Please forgive me. Please.

So I've been here. Alone again. In this large man-made desert. I have nobody left. So I will put on my dad's bandana. Eat one last meal. Then I'm going to end it. I'm going to put this .40 caliber in my mouth and pull the trigger.

So whoever finds this journal, I hope you know that we are all human. Whether you find this and the world is worse, and people are killing each other for simple survival; or perhaps mankind will learn to work together again and rebuild what's left. Know that I tried to be decent. Know that mankind was not meant to be savage. I hope that the threat of these dead heads eventually die out. That mankind becomes good stewards of the earth again.

But it's hard for me to believe in fairy tales anymore. Any happy endings. If I close my eyes, I can almost picture our old house. Mom and dad, Leigh, me and our dog jack. Sitting in the backyard with a fire going. Dad would be roasting marshmallows while mom would put the s'mores together. I can almost hear the crickets in the yard and the frogs croaking in the swamp behind our house.

Sometimes, dad would bring out his guitar and sing some silly song that he made up off the top of his head. We'd all laugh and try to sing our own dumb verses...

ABOUT THE AUTHOR

Bradley L. Bodeker was born in Honolulu, Hawaii. He has published his poetry in two books *reflectshuns in a broken mirror* and *another shard of glass*. Both of which have been collected and unabridged in *The Broken Mirror Reflected*. His first horror anthology *Midnight Snacks* and his bestselling *Zechariah 14:12-humanity's last stand* have also been published.

He has written numerous commercials for radio, acted in several musicals including the lead role in *Shrek* in southern MN. He currently resides on the outskirts of the Twin Cities on a hobby farm with 2 dogs, a cat, 7 goats, a rabbit, 6 chickens and 5 ducks.

http://themadproet.weebly.com
Like me on facebook/b-hive-productions

CPSIA information can be obtained
at www.ICGtesting.com
Printed in the USA
LVHW080758301119
638727LV00025BA/3442/P